D0708595

AUTHOR

TITLE

CLASS SF   F

Michael Moorcock is astonishing. His enormous output includes around fifty novels, innumerable short stories and a rock album. Born in London in 1939, he became editor of *Tarzan Adventures* at sixteen, moving on later to edit the *Sexton Blake Library*. He has earned his living as a writer/editor ever since, and is without doubt one of Britain's most popular and most prolific authors. He has been compared with Tennyson, Tolkien, Raymond Chandler, Wyndham Lewis, Ronald Firbank, Mervyn Peake, Edgar Allan Poe, Colin Wilson, Anatole France, William Burroughs, Edgar Rice Burroughs, Charles Dickens, James Joyce, Vladimir Nabokov, Jorge Luis Borges, Joyce Cary, Ray Bradbury, H. G. Wells, George Bernard Shaw and Hieronymus Bosch, among others.

'No one at the moment in England is doing more to break down the artificial divisions that have grown up in novel writing – realism, surrealism, science fiction, historical fiction, social satire, the poetic novel – than Michael Moorcock'
Angus Wilson

'He is an ingenious and energetic experimenter, restlessly original, brimming over with clever ideas'
Robert Nye, *The Guardian*

By the same author

MICHAEL MOORCOCK

The Quest for Tanelorn

The third and final volume of
The Chronicles of Castle Brass:
a sequel to the High History of the Runestaff

GRAFTON BOOKS

A Division of the Collins Publishing Group

LONDON GLASGOW
TORONTO SYDNEY AUCKLAND

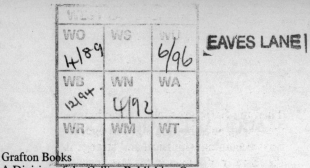

Grafton Books
A Division of the Collins Publishing Group
8 Grafton Street, London W1X 3LA

Published by Grafton Books 1988

Previously published as a Mayflower Original 1975
Reprinted 1976, 1977, 1980, 1982

Copyright © Michael Moorcock 1975

ISBN 0-586-20533-0

Printed and bound in Great Britain by
Collins, Glasgow

Set in Plantin

Then the Earth grew old, its landscapes mellowing and showing signs of age, its ways becoming whimsical and strange in the manner of a man in his last years.

– The High History of the Runestaff

And when this History was done there followed it another. A Romance involving the same participants in experiences perhaps even more bizarre and awesome than the last. And again the ancient Castle of Brass in the marshy Kamarg was the centre for much of this action . . .

– The Chronicles of Castle Brass

CONTENTS

BOOK ONE

THE WORLD INSANE:
A CHAMPION OF DREAMS

1

AN OLD FRIEND AT CASTLE BRASS

'Lost?'

'Aye.'

'But only dreams, Hawkmoon. Lost dreams?' The tone was nearly pathetic.

'I think not.'

Count Brass moved his great body away from the window so that light fell suddenly on Hawkmoon's gaunt face. 'Would that I had two grandchildren. Would that I had. Perhaps one day . . .'

It was a conversation which had been repeated so many times that it had become almost a ritual. Count Brass did not like mysteries; he did not respect them.

'There was a boy and a girl.' Hawkmoon was still tired, but there was no longer any madness in him. 'Manfred and Yarmila. The boy much resembled you.'

'We have told you this, father.' Yisselda, hands folded under her breasts, moved from the shade near the fireplace. She wore a green gown, cuffs and collar ermine-trimmed. Her hair was drawn back from her face. She was pale. She had been pale since her return, with Hawkmoon, to Castle Brass, more than a month ago. 'We told you – and we must find them.'

Count Brass ran heavy fingers through his greying red hair, his red brows furrowed. 'I did not believe Hawkmoon – but I believe you both now, though I do not wish to.'

'It is why you argue so, father.' Yisselda placed a hand upon his brocaded arm.

'Bowgentle could explain these paradoxes, possibly,' Count Brass continued, 'but there is no other who could

3

find the kind of words which a plain-thinking soldier like myself could easily understand. You are of the belief that I have been brought back from the dead, yet I've no memory of dying. And Yisselda has been rescued from Limbo, when I, myself, thought her slain at the Battle of Londra. Now you speak of children, also somewhere in Limbo. A horrifying thought. Children experiencing such terrors! Ah! No! I will not consider it.'

'We have had to, Count Brass.' Hawkmoon spoke with the authority of a man who had faced many hours alone with his darkest thoughts. 'It is why we are determined to do everything we can to find them. It is why, today, we leave for Londra where we hope Queen Flana and her scientists can help us.'

Count Brass fingered his thick red moustaches. The mention of Londra had aroused other thoughts in his mind. There was a slight expression of embarrassment on his face. He cleared his throat.

There was kindly humour in Yisselda's eyes as she said, 'Is there a message we can give Queen Flana?'

Her father shrugged. 'The usual courtesies, of course. I intend to write. Perhaps I will have time to give you a letter before you leave.'

'She would be glad to see you in person again.' Yisselda glanced meaningly at Hawkmoon, who rubbed at the back of his neck. 'In her last letter she told me how much she had enjoyed your visit, father. She remarked on the wisdom of your counsel, the practical common sense of your advice in matters of State. There was a hint that she could offer you an official position at the Court of Londra.'

Count Brass's ruddy features seemed to take on a deeper shade of colour, a blush. 'She mentioned something of that. But she does not need me in Londra.'

'Not for your advice, certainly,' said Yisselda. 'Your support . . .? She was fond of men, once. But with D'Averc's terrible death – I have heard that she has had no

4

thoughts of marrying. I have heard that she has considered the question of an heir, but that there is only one man who could, in her opinion, compare with Huillam D'Averc. I speak clumsily . . .'

'Indeed you do, daughter. It is understandable, for your mind is full of other thoughts. I am touched, however, by your willingness to concern yourself with my very minor affairs.' Count Brass smiled and put his arm out to Yisselda. The brocade sleeve fell away to reveal his bronzed, heavily muscled forearm. 'But I am too old to marry. If I planned marriage, certainly I could think of no better wife than Flana. But the decision I made many years ago to live in virtual retirement in the Kamarg remains. Besides, I have my duty to the folk of the Kamarg. Would I abandon that?'

'We could take up that duty, as we did once when you were . . .' She paused.

'Dead?' Count Brass frowned. 'I am grateful that I do not have such memories of you, Yisselda. When I returned from Londra and found you here I was full of joy. I asked for no explanation. It was enough that you lived. But then, I had seen you die at Londra some years before. It was a memory I was happy to doubt. A memory of children, though – to be haunted by such ghosts, by the knowledge that they are alive somewhere and afraid – Oh, that is terrifying!'

'It is a familiar terror,' said Hawkmoon. 'Hopefully we shall find them. Hopefully they know nothing of all this. Hopefully, in whatever other plane they now inhabit, they are happy.'

There came a knock on the door of Count Brass's study. He answered it in his gruff voice: 'Enter.'

Captain Josef Vedla opened the door, closed it behind him and stood in silence for a moment. The old soldier was clad in what he chose to call his civilian clothing – doeskin shirt, buckskin jerkin and breeks, boots of old, black leather. At his belt was a long dirk, apparently there not for any particular usefulness save to act as a familiar rest for his left hand. 'The ornithopter is almost ready,' he said. 'It will take you to Karlye. The Silver Bridge is completed, rebuilt in all its old beauty, and by means of it you may cross, Duke Dorian, as you wished, to Deau-Vere.'

'Thank you, Captain Vedla. It will please me to make this journey from the Kamarg by the route I used when I first came to Castle Brass.'

Her hand still in that of her father, Yisselda stretched her other hand out and took Hawkmoon's. Her steady eyes regarded his face and her grip tightened for a second on his fingers. He drew a deep breath. 'Then we must go,' he said.

'There was other news . . .' Josef Vedla hesitated.

'Other news?'

'Of a rider, sir. He has been seen by our guardians. We received a heliograph message a few minutes ago. He comes towards the town . . .'

'Has he announced himself at our borders?' Count Brass asked.

'That is what is strange, Count Brass. He was not seen at the borders. He was half-way into the Kamarg before he was sighted.'

'That is unusual. Our guardians are normally vigilant . . .'

'They are quite as vigilant today. He did not enter by any of the known roads.'

'Well, doubtless we'll have the opportunity of asking him how he avoided being seen,' said Yisselda calmly. 'After all, it is one rider, not an army.'

Hawkmoon laughed. For a moment they had all been over-worried. 'Have him met, Captain Vedla. Invite him to the castle.'

Vedla saluted and left.

Hawkmoon went to the window and looked over the roofs of Aigues-Mortes to the fields and lagoons beyond the old town. The sky was a clear, pale blue and the distant water reflected it. A light, winter wind was blowing at the reed beds. He saw a movement on the wide, white road that came through the marshes to the town. He saw the rider. He was coming swiftly, at a steady canter, sitting upright in his saddle, sitting proudly, it seemed to Hawkmoon. And the rider's outline was familiar. Rather than peer at the distant figure, Hawkmoon turned away from the window, prepared to wait until it was closer and could be identified easily.

'An old friend – or an old enemy,' he said. 'I recognize something about his stance.'

'We have had no announcement,' said Count Brass. He shrugged. 'But these are not the old days. These are calmer times.'

'For some,' said Hawkmoon, then he regretted the self-pity in his tone. He had had too much of such emotions. Now that he was rid of them he was, perhaps, overly sensitive to any traces of their return he detected in himself. From an over-indulgence in such feelings, he had now gone to a mood of intense stoicism which was a relief to all save those who knew him best and had the greatest affection for him. Sensitive to his thoughts, Yisselda reached to place delicate fingers upon his lips and then his cheek. Gratefully, he smiled at her, drawing her to him and kissing her lightly upon the forehead.

'Now I must prepare for our journey,' she said.

Hawkmoon was already dressed in the clothes in which he intended to travel.

'Will you and father wait here to receive our visitor?' she asked Hawkmoon.

He nodded. 'I think so. There is always hope that . . .'

'Do not expect it, my dear. There is little chance that he will bring news of Manfred and Yarmila.'

7

'True.'

With another smile at her father, Yisselda left the room.

Count Brass strode to a table of polished oak on which a tray had been set. He lifted a pewter jug. 'Would you share a glass of wine with me, Hawkmoon, before you go?'

'Thank you.'

Hawkmoon joined Count Brass at the table, accepting the carved wooden goblet the old warrior handed him. He sipped the wine and resisted the temptation to return to the window to see if he recognized the traveller.

'More than ever, I regret that Bowgentle is not here to advise us,' said Count Brass. 'All this talk of other planes of existence, of other possibilities, of dead friends still alive – it smacks of the occult. All my life I have looked with a cold eye upon superstitions; I have scoffed at pseudo-philosophical speculation. But I have not the kind of mind which can easily distinguish between mumbo-jumbo and that which falls into the province of the genuinely metaphysical.'

'Do not misinterpret what I say as morbid brooding,' Hawkmoon replied, 'but I have reason to hope that Bowgentle may, one day, be restored to us.'

'The difference between us, I suppose,' said Count Brass, 'is that you, for all your rediscovered toughness of mind, continue to allow yourself to entertain many forms of hope. Long ago, I dismissed Faith altogether – at least from my conscious thoughts. Yet you, Hawkmoon, discover it over and over again.'

'Aye – through many lives.'

'What?'

'I refer to my dreams. To those strange dreams of myself in so many different incarnations. I had identified those dreams with my madness, but now I am not so sure. They still come to me, you know.'

'You have not mentioned them since you returned here with Yisselda.'

8

'They have not tormented me as they once did. But they are familiar, still.'

'Every night?'

'Aye. Every night. The names – Elric, Erekosë, Corum – those are the chief ones. And there are others. And sometimes I see the Runestaff, and sometimes a black sword. All seem significant. And sometimes, when I am alone, particularly when I ride the marshlands, they come to me in my waking hours. Faces, familiar and unfamiliar, float before me. Snatches of words are heard. And most common is that frightening phrase "Champion Eternal" . . . Formerly I would have thought that only a madman could think of himself as a demigod . . .'

'I, too,' said Count Brass, pouring more wine for Hawkmoon. 'But it is others who make their heroes into demigods. Would that the world had no need for heroes.'

'A sane world will not need them.'

'But perhaps a sane world is a world without human-kind.' Count Brass's smile was bleak. 'Perhaps it is we who make it what it is?'

'If an individual can make himself whole, so can our race,' said Hawkmoon. 'If I have Faith, Count Brass, that is why I retain it.'

'I wish that I shared such Faith. I see Man as destined, ultimately, to self-destruction. All that I hope for is that that destiny can be averted for as long as possible, that Man's most foolish actions can be restrained, that a little equilibrium can be maintained.'

'Equilibrium. The idea symbolized by the Cosmic Balance, by the Runestaff. Have I told you that I have come to doubt that philosophy? Have I told you that I have come to the conclusion that equilibrium is not enough – not in the sense you mean? Equilibrium in an individual is a fine thing – a balance between the needs of the mind and the needs of the body – maintained without self-consciousness. Certainly, let us aim for that. But what of the world? Would we tame it too much?'

'You have lost me, my friend.' Count Brass laughed. 'I was never a cautious man, in the ordinary sense of the word, but I became a weary one. Perhaps it is weariness which now informs your thoughts?'

'It is anger,' said Hawkmoon. 'We served the Runestaff. It cost us dear to serve it. Many died. Many were tormented. We still know a terrible despair. And we were told that we could call on its help when we needed it. Do we not need it now?'

'Perhaps we do not need it enough.'

Hawkmoon's laugh was grim. 'If you are right, I do not look forward much to a future when we *shall* need it enough!'

And then his head was filled by a revelation and he rushed to the window. But by now the figure had left the road and entered the town and could not be seen. 'I know that rider!'

There came a knock at the door. Hawkmoon went to it and flung it open.

And there he stood, tall and cocky and proud, with his hand on his hip and the heel of his other hand resting on the pommel of his plain sword, a folded cloak over his right shoulder, his bonnet at a tilt and a crooked grin on his red, raw face. It was the Orkneyman, the brother of the Warrior in Jet and Gold. It was Orland Fank, Servant of the Runestaff.

'Good day to ye, Duke of Köln,' he said.

Hawkmoon's brow was furrowed and his smile was bleak. 'Good day to you, Master Fank. Do you come asking favours?'

'The folk of Orkney ask nothing for nothing, Duke Dorian.'

'And the Runestaff – what does that ask?'

Orland Fank took a few paces into the room, Captain Vedla at his heels. He stood beside the fire and warmed his hands at it, glancing about him. There was sardonic amusement in his eyes, as if he relished their puzzlement.

'I thank ye for sending your emissary here with your invitation to guest at Castle Brass,' said Fank, winking up at Vedla, who was disconcerted still. 'I was not sure how ye'd receive me.'

'You were right to wonder, Master Fank.' Hawkmoon's own expression matched Fank's. 'I seem to remember something of an oath you swore, when we parted. Since then we have battled dangers quite as momentous as those we fought in the service of the Runestaff – and the Runestaff has been not one wit in evidence.'

Fank frowned. 'Aye, that's true. But blame neither myself nor the staff for that. Those forces affecting you and yours also affected the Runestaff. It is gone from this world, Hawkmoon of Köln. I have sought it in Amarehk, in Asiacommunista, in all the lands of this Earth. Then I heard rumours of your madness – of peculiar happenings here in the Kamarg – and I came, barely stopping, all the way from the Courts of Muskovia to visit you and ask you if you have an explanation for the events of the past year or so.'

'You – the Runestaff's oracle – come to ask us for information?' Count Brass let forth a bellow of laughter and slapped at his thigh. 'Oh, this is indeed a turning world!'

'I have information to exchange!' Fank drew himself up to face Count Brass, his back to the fire, his hand on his sword's hilt. All his amusement was suddenly gone from him and Hawkmoon noticed how drawn his face seemed, how tired his eyes were.

Hawkmoon poured out a cup of wine and handed it swiftly to Fank who accepted it, flashing Hawkmoon a quick glance of gratitude.

Count Brass regretted his outburst and his expression became sober. 'I am sorry, Master Fank. I am a poor

11

host.'

'And I a poor guest, count. I see from the activity in your courtyard that someone leaves Castle Brass today.'

'Yisselda and I go to Londra,' said Hawkmoon.

'Yisselda? So it is true. I heard different tales – that Yisselda was dead, that Count Brass was dead – and I could not deny or confirm them, for I found my memory playing peculiar tricks. I lost confidence in my own recollection of events . . .'

'We have all had that experience,' said Hawkmoon. And he told Fank of everything he could remember (it was garbled, there were some things he could only half remember, some things he could only guess at) concerning his recent adventures, which seemed to him unreal, and his recent dreams which seemed much more tangible. Fank continued to stand before the fire, his hands behind his back, his head upon his chest, listening with absolute concentration to every word. Occasionally he would nod, sometimes he would grunt, and very rarely he would ask for clarification of some phrase. While he listened, Yisselda, dressed in heavy jerkin and breeks for her journey, entered, and seated herself silently by the window, only speaking when, towards the end of Hawkmoon's account, she could add information of her own.

'It is true,' she said, when Hawkmoon had finished. 'The dreams seem the reality, and the reality seems the dream. Can you explain that, Master Fank?'

Fank sniffed, rubbing at his nose. 'There are many versions of reality, my lady. Some would say that our dreams reflect events in other planes. There is a great disruption taking place, but I do not think it was caused by the experiments of Kalan and Taragorm. As far as their work goes, I think the damage has been largely repaired. I think they were able to exploit this larger disruption for a while. Possibly they exacerbated the condition, but that is all. Their efforts were puny. They could not have caused all this. I suspect a vaster conflict. I suspect that there are forces at work so huge and terrifying that the Runestaff has been called from this individual plane to serve in a war of which we have received only a hint. A great war in which the destiny of the planes will be fixed for a period of time most would consider Eternity. I speak of something I know little about, my friends. I have only heard the phrase "The Conjunction of the Million Spheres", spoken by a dying philosopher in the mountains of Asiacommunista. Means the phrase anything to you?'

The phrase was familiar to Hawkmoon, yet he was sure he had not heard it before, even in his strange dreams. He told Fank that.

'I had hoped ye'd know more, Duke Dorian. But I believe that phrase to have considerable significance to us all. Now I learn that ye seek lost children, while I seek the Runestaff. What of the word "Tanelorn"? Means that anything?'

'A city,' said Hawkmoon. 'The name of a city.'

'Aye. That is what I heard. Yet I have found no city of that name anywhere in this world. It must lie in some other. Would we find the Runestaff there? Would we find your children there?'

'In Tanelorn?'

'In Tanelorn.'

2

ON THE SILVER BRIDGE

Fank had elected to remain at Castle Brass and so Hawkmoon and Yisselda climbed into the cushioned cabin of the great ornithopter. Ahead, in his small, open cockpit, the pilot began to manipulate the controls.

Count Brass and Fank stood outside the door of the castle watching as the heavy metallic wings began to beat and the strange motors of the ancient craft murmured, whispered and crooned. There came a fluttering of enamelled silver feathers, a lurch, a wind which set Count Brass's red hair pouring back from his head and caused Orland Fank to hang on to his bonnet; then the ornithopter began to rise.

Count Brass raised a hand in farewell. The machine banked a little as it rose over the red and yellow roofs of the town, then it wheeled once, turned to avoid a cloud of wild, giant flamingos which blossomed suddenly from one of the lagoons to the west, gained height and speed with each beat of its clashing wings, and soon it seemed to Hawkmoon and Yisselda that they were entirely sur-rounded by the cold, lovely blue of the winter sky.

Since their conversation with Orland Fank, Hawkmoon had been in a thoughtful mood and Yisselda, respecting this mood, had made no attempt to talk to him. Now he turned to her, smiling gently.

'There are still wise men in Londra,' he said. 'Queen Flana's court has attracted many scholars, many philo-sophers. Perhaps some will be able to help us.'

'You know of Tanelorn?' she said. 'The city Fank mentioned.'

'Only the name. I feel I *should* know much. I feel that I

have been there, at least once, possibly many times, yet you and I both know that I have not.'

'In your dreams? Have you been there in your dreams, Dorian?'

He shrugged. 'Sometimes it seems to me that I have been everywhere in my dreams – in every age of the Earth – even beyond the Earth and to other worlds. I am convinced of one thing; that there are a thousand other Earths, even a thousand other galaxies – and that events in our world are mirrored in all the rest; that the same destinies are played out in subtly different ways. But whether those destinies are controlled by ourselves or by other, superhuman, forces, I do not know. Are there such things as Gods, Yisselda?'

'Men make Gods. Bowgentle once offered the opinion that the mind of Man is so powerful that it can make "real" anything it desperately needs to be real.'

'And perhaps those other worlds are real because, at some time in our history, enough people needed them. Could that be how alternative worlds are created?'

She shrugged. 'It is not something you and I are likely to prove, no matter how much information we are given.'

Tacitly, they both dropped this line of thought, contenting themselves with the magnificence of the views which passed below them as they peered through the portholes of the cabin. Steadily the ornithopter headed northward to the coasts, at length passing over the tinkling towers of Parye, the Crystal City, now restored in all its finery. The sunlight was reflected and transformed into rainbow colours by the scores of prisms, the spires of Parye, created by means of that city's timeless and cryptic technologies. They observed whole buildings, gilded and ancient, wholly enclosed in vast, apparently solid eight-, ten-, and twelve-sided crystal structures.

Half blinded, they fell back from the portholes, still able to see the sky all around them filled with soft, pulsating colours, still able to hear the gentle, musical ringing of the glass ornaments which the citizens of Parye used to decorate their quartz-paved streets. Even the warlords of the Dark Empire had let Parye stand; even those insane and bloody-handed destroyers had held the Crystal City in awe – and now she was fully restored to all her great beauty and it was said that the children of Parye were born blind, that it was often three years before their eyes were capable of accepting the everyday visions granted to those who habitually dwelled therein.

Parye behind them, they now entered grey cloud and the pilot, kept warm by the heater in his cockpit and the thick flying garments he wore, sought clearer sky above the cloud, found none, and dropped lower until they were barely two hundred feet from the flat, dull winter fields of the country lying inland from Karlye. A light drizzle was falling and, as the drizzle turned to driving rain, the sun began to set, so that they came to Karlye at dusk, seeing the warm lights welcoming them from the windows of the city's cobblestone buildings. They circled over Karlye's quaintly designed roof tops of dark red and light grey slates, dropping, at length, into the bowl of the circular, grass-sown, landing field around which the city was built. For an ornithopter (never the most comfortable of flying machines) the vessel landed smoothly, with Hawkmoon and Yisselda clinging firmly to the straps provided until the bumping had stopped and the pilot, his transparent visor streaming with moisture, turned to indicate to them that they might leave. The rain beat heavily now upon the cabin's canopy and Hawkmoon and Yisselda dressed themselves in thick capes which covered them to their feet. Across the landing field men came running, bodies bent into the wind, and behind them was a hand-drawn carriage. Hawkmoon waited until the carriage had been positioned as close as possible to the ornithopter, then he drew open the oddly shaped door and helped Yisselda to cross the sodden ground to the vehicle. They climbed in, and with a rather exaggerated lurch, the carriage moved towards the buildings on the far side of the field.

'We'll lodge in Karlye tonight,' said Hawkmoon, 'and leave early in the morning for the Silver Bridge.'

Count Brass's agents in Karlye had already secured rooms for the Duke of Köln and Yisselda of Brass; these were situated not far from the landing field, in a small but extremely comfortable inn which was one of the few buildings to have survived the conquerings of the Dark Empire. Yisselda remembered that she had stayed here with her father when she was a child and at first she felt a simple delight until her own childhood reminded her of her lost Yarmila, and then her brow became clouded. Hawkmoon, realizing what had happened, put his arm around her shoulders to comfort her when, after eating a good supper, they went upstairs to bed.

The day had tired them and neither was of a disposition to stay awake talking, for there was little left to talk about, so they slept.

But Hawkmoon's sleep was almost immediately populated by his all too familiar dreams – faces and images jostling for his attention – eyes imploring him, hands beseeching him, as if a whole world, perhaps a whole universe, cried out for his attention and his aid.

And he was Corum – alien Corum of the Vadhagh – riding against the foul Fhoi Myore, the Cold Folk from Limbo . . .

And he was Elric – Last Prince of Melniboné – a shouting battleblade in his right hand, his left upon the pommel of an oddly wrought saddle, the saddle on the back of a huge reptilian monster whose saliva turned to fire wherever it dripped . . .

And he was Erekosë – poor Erekosë – leading the Eldren to victory over his own human people – And he was Urlik Skarsol Prince of the Southern Ice, crying out in despair at his fate, which was to bear the Black Sword . . .

TANELORN . . .

Oh, where was Tanelorn . . .?

Had he not been there, at least once? Did he not recall a sense of absolute peace of mind, of wholeness of spirit, of the happiness only those who have suffered profoundly may feel?

TANELORN . . .

'*Too long have I borne my burden – too long have I paid the price of Erekosë's great crime . . .*' *It was his voice which spoke, but it was not his lips which formed the words – they were other lips, unhuman lips . . .* '*I must have rest – I must have rest . . .*'

And now there came a face – a face of ineffable evil, but it was not a confident face – a dark face – was it desperate? Was it his face? Was this his face, too?

AH, I SUFFER!

This way and that, the familiar armies marched. Familiar swords rose and fell. Familiar faces screamed and perished, and blood flowed from body after body – a familiar flowing . . .

TANELORN – have I not earned the peace of Tanelorn? Not yet, Champion. Not yet . . .

It is unjust that I, alone, should suffer so!

You do not suffer alone. Mankind suffers with you.

It is unjust!

Then make justice!

I cannot. I am only a man.

You are the Champion. You are the Eternal Champion.

I am a man!

You are a man. You are the Champion Eternal.

I am only a man!

You are only the Champion.

I am Elric! I am Urlik! I am Erekosë! I am Corum! I am too many. I am too many!

You are one.

And now, in his dreams (if dreams they were), Hawkmoon felt, for a brief instant, a sense of peace, an understanding too profound for words. He was one. He was one . . .

But then it was gone and he was many again. And he yelled in his bed and he begged for peace.

And Yisselda was clinging to his threshing body. And Yisselda was weeping. And light fell on his face from the window. It was dawn.

'Dorian. Dorian. Dorian.'

'Yisselda.'

He drew a deep beath. 'Oh, Yisselda.' And he was grateful that at least she had not been taken from him, for he had no other consolation but her in all the world, in all the many worlds he experienced while he slept; so he held her close to him in his strong warrior's arms, and he wept for a little while, and she wept with him. Then they rose from the bed and dressed themselves and in silence they left the inn without breakfasting, mounting the good horses which waited for them. They rode away from Karlye, along the coast road, through the rain which swept from the grey, turbulent sea, until they came to the Silver Bridge which spanned thirty miles of water between the mainland and the isle of Granbretan.

The Silver Bridge was not as Hawkmoon had seen it, all those many years before. Its tall pylons, obscured now by mist, by rain, and, at their tops, by cloud, no longer bore motifs of warfare and Dark Empire glories; instead they were decorated with designs supplied by all the cities of the continent which the Dark Empire warlords had once pillaged – a great variety of designs, celebrating the harmony of Nature. The vast causeway still measured a quarter of a mile wide, but previously, when Hawkmoon had crossed it, it had carried war-machines, the loot of a hundred great campaigns, the beast-warriors of the Dark Empire. Now trading caravans came and went along its two main roads; travellers from Normandia, from Italia, Slavia, Rolance, Scandia, from the Bulgar Mountains, from the great German city-states, from Pesht and from Ulm, from Wien, from Krahkov and even from distant, mysterious Muskovia. There were waggons drawn by horses, by oxen, by elephants, even. There were trains of camels, mules and donkeys. There were carts propelled by mechanical devices, often faulty, often faltering, whose principles were understood by only a handful of clever men and women (and most of them could understand only in the abstract) but which had worked for a thousand years or more; there were men on horseback and there were men who had walked hundreds of miles to cross the wonder that was the Silver Bridge. Clothing was often outlandish, some of it dull, patched, dusty, some of it vulgar in its magnificence. Furs, leather, silks, plaids, the skins of strange beasts, the feathers of rare birds, decorated the heads and backs of the travellers, and some who were clad in the greatest finery suffered the most in the chill rain which soaked through the subtly dyed fabrics and quickly found the unadorned flesh beneath. Hawkmoon and Yisselda travelled in heavy, warm gear that was plain, bereft of any decoration, but their steeds were sturdy and carried them without tiring, and soon they had joined the throng heading westward towards a land once feared by all but now transformed, under Queen Flana, into a centre of art and trade and learning and just government. There would have been several quicker ways of reaching Londra, but Hawkmoon's desire was strong to reach the city by the same means he had first left it.

His spirits improved as he looked at the quivering hawsers supporting the main causeway, at the intricate workmanship of the silversmiths who had fashioned decorations many inches thick to cover the strong steel of the pylons which had been built not only to bear millions of tons in weight but also to withstand the perpetual pounding of the waves, the pressure of the deepest currents so far beneath the surface. Here was a monument to what man could achieve, both useful and beautiful, without need of supernatural agencies of any sort. All his life he had despised that sad and insecure philosophy which argued that man, alone, was not great enough to achieve marvels, that he must be controlled by some superhuman force (gods, more sophisticated intelligences from somewhere beyond the Solar System) to have achieved what he had achieved. Only those frightened of the power within their own minds could have need of such views, thought Hawkmoon, noticing that the sky was clearing and a little sunlight was beginning to touch the silver hawsers and make them glint more brightly than before. He drew in a deep breath of the ozone-laden air, smiling as gulls wheeled about the upper levels of the pylons, pointing out the sails of a ship just before it passed under the bridge and beyond their view, commenting on the beauty of a particular bas-relief, the originality of a particular piece of silver-work. Both he and Yisselda became calmer as they took an interest in all the sights and they spoke of the pleasure they would experience if Londra were half as beautiful as this reborn bridge.

And then it seemed to Hawkmoon that a silence fell upon the Silver Bridge, that the clatter of the waggons and the hooves of the beasts disappeared, that the crying of the gulls ceased, that the sound of the waves went away, and he turned to mention this to Yisselda and she had gone. And he looked about him and he realized, in dawning terror, that he was quite alone on the bridge.

There was a thin cry from very far away – a cry which might have been Yisselda calling to him – then that, too, was gone.

And Hawkmoon made to wheel his horse about, to ride back the way he had come in the hope that, if he moved swiftly, he could rejoin Yisselda.

But Hawkmoon's horse refused to be handled. It was snorting. It stamped at the metal of the bridge. It whinneyed.

And Hawkmoon, betrayed, screamed a single, agonized word.

'NO!'

3

IN THE MIST

'No!'

It was another voice – a booming, pain-racked voice, far louder than Hawkmoon's, louder than thunder.

And the bridge swayed and the horse reared and Hawkmoon was thrown heavily to the metal causeway. He tried to rise; he tried to crawl back to where he was sure he would find Yisselda.

'Yisselda!' he cried.

'Yisselda!'

And wicked laughter sounded behind him.

He turned his head, lying spreadeagled on the swaying bridge. He saw his horse, its eyes rolling, tumble over, slide to the edge, to be pinned against a rail, its legs kicking at the air.

Now Hawkmoon tried to reach for the sword beneath his cloak, but he could not free it. It was pinned beneath him.

The laughter came again, but its pitch and its tone changed; it was less confident. Then the voice gave out its bellowing echo:

'No!'

Hawkmoon knew a terrible fear, a fear greater than anything he had previously confronted. His impulse was to crawl away from the source of that fear, but he forced himself to turn his head again and look at the face.

The face filled his whole horizon, glaring out of the mist which swirled around the swaying bridge. The dark face of his dreams, its eyes were filled with glaring menace, with a complicated terror of its own, and the huge lips formed the word which was a challenge, a command, a plea:

'No!'

Then Hawkmoon climbed to his feet and stood with his legs apart, balancing himself, staring back at the face, staring by virtue of an effort of will which astonished him.

'Who are you?' said Hawkmoon. His voice was thin, the mist seemed to absorb the words. 'Who are you? Who are you?'

'No!'

The face was apparently without a body. It was beautiful and sinister and of a dark, indeterminate colour. The lips were a glowing unhealthy red; the eyes were perhaps black, perhaps blue, perhaps brown, and there was a kind of gold in the pupils.

Hawkmoon knew that the creature was in torment, but he knew, too, that it menaced him, that it would destroy him if it could. Again his hand went to his sword, but fell away as he realized how useless the blade would be, what an empty gesture it would be if he drew it.

'SWORD . . .' said the being. 'SWORD . . .' The word had considerable meaning. 'SWORD . . .' Once again its tone changed, to that of an unrequited lover, pleading for the return of the object of its love and hating itself for its wretchedness, hating, too, that which it loved. There was a threat in its voice; there was death there.

'ELRIC? URLIK? ME . . . I WAS A THOUSAND . . . ELRIC? ME . . .?'

Was this some fearful manifestation of the Champion Eternal – of Hawkmoon himself? Did he look upon his own soul?

'ME . . . THE TIME . . . THE CONJUNCTION . . . I CAN HELP . . .'

Hawkmoon dismissed the thought. It was possible that the being represented something within himself, but it was not the whole of him. He knew that it had a separate identity and he knew, also, that it needed flesh, it needed form, and that was what he could give it. Not his own

24

flesh, but something which was his.

'Who are you?' Hawkmoon felt strength enter his voice as he forced himself to look upon the dark, glaring face.

'ME . . .'

The eyes focused on Hawkmoon and they glowed with hatred. Hawkmoon's instinct was to step backward, but he held his ground and returned the glare of those evil, gigantic eyes. The lips snarled and revealed jagged, flaming teeth. Hawkmoon trembled.

Words came to Hawkmoon and he spoke them firmly, though he did not know their origin, or their import, only that they were the right words.

'You must go,' he said. 'You have no place here.'

'I MUST SURVIVE – THE CONJUNCTION – YOU WILL SURVIVE WITH ME, ELRIC . . .'

'I am not Elric.'

'YOU ARE ELRIC!'

'I am Hawkmoon.'

'WHAT OF IT? A MERE NAME. IT IS AS ELRIC THAT I LOVE YOU MOST. I HAVE HELPED YOU SO WELL . . .'

'You mean to destroy me,' said Hawkmoon, 'that I do know. I'll accept no help from you. It is your help which has chained me through millennia. It will be the last action of the Champion Eternal to take part in your destruction!'

'YOU KNOW ME?'

'Not yet. Fear the time when I *shall* know you!'

'ME . . .'

'You must go. I begin to recognize you.'

'NO!'

'You must go.' Hawkmoon felt his voice begin to quaver and he doubted if he could look upon that terrible face for another moment.

'Me . . .' The voice was fainter, it threatened less, it pleaded more.

'You must go.'

'Me . . .'

Then Hawkmoon summoned all that remained of his will and he laughed at it.

'Go!'

Hawkmoon spread his arms wide as he began to fall, for face and bridge had vanished at the same moment.

He fell through chilling mist, head over heels, his cloak flapping about him and tangling itself in his legs – through chilling mist and into cold water. He gasped. His mouth filled with the salt of the sea. He coughed and his lungs were full of shards of ice. He forced the water out, striking upwards, trying to reach the surface. He began to drown.

His body heaved as it tried to draw in air and force out water, but there was only water for it to breath. Once he opened his eyes and saw his hands, and his hands were the bone-white hands of a corpse; white hair drifted about his face. He knew his name was no longer Hawkmoon, so he closed his eyes tight shut again and repeated his old battle cry, the battle cry of his ancestors which he had voiced a hundred times in his wars against the Dark Empire.

Hawkmoon . . . Hawkmoon . . . Hawkmoon . . .

'Hawkmoon!'

This was not his own shout. It came from above him, from out of the mist. He forced his body to the surface. He blew the water from his lungs. He gasped at the freezing air.

'Hawkmoon!'

There was a dark outline on the surface of the ocean. There was a regular splashing sound.

'Here!' cried Hawkmoon.

The small rowing boat came slowly towards him, its oars rising and falling. A small figure sat in it. He was swathed in a heavy sea-cloak, there was a wide-brimmed, dripping hat obscuring the greater part of his features, but the grin on his lips was unmistakable, and unmistakable, too, was his companion who sat in the prow of the boat looking with apparent concern in its yellow eyes at Hawkmoon. It was a very wet little creature, that black and white cat. It spread its wings once, to shake moisture from them. It mewed.

Hawkmoon clutched the wooden side of the boat and Jhary-a-Conel methodically shipped his oars before reaching carefully down to help the Duke of Köln aboard.

'It is wise for such as me to trust to his instincts,' said Jhary-a-Conel, handing Hawkmoon a flask of some strong spirit. 'Do you know where we are, Dorian Hawkmoon?'

Unable to speak for the water still in his lungs and stomach, Hawkmoon lay back in the boat and shivered and vomited while Jhary-a-Conel, self-styled Companion to Heroes, began once more to row.

'I thought it first a river, then a lake,' said Jhary conversationally, 'then I decided it must be a sea. You have swallowed a great deal of it. What do you say?'

Hawkmoon spat the last of the water over the side. He wondered at his impulse to laugh. 'A sea,' he said. 'How came you to be boating on it?'

'An impulse.' Jhary seemed to notice the small black and white cat for the first time and showed surprise. 'Aha! So I am Jhary-a-Conel, am I?'

'You were uncertain?'

'I think I had another name when I began to row. Then the mist came.' Jhary shrugged. 'No matter. For me, it's a familiar enough event. Well, well, Hawkmoon, how came you to be *swimming* in this sea?'

'I fell from a bridge,' said Hawkmoon simply, not wishing, for the moment, to discuss the experience. He did not bother to ask Jhary-a-Conel whether they were nearer to France or to Granbretan, particularly since it was just beginning to dawn on him that he had no business remembering Jhary's name or feeling such a close familiarity with him. 'I met you in the Bulgar Mountains, did I not? With Katinka van Bak?'

27

'I seem to recall something of that. You were Ilian of Garathorm for a while, then Hawkmoon again. How swiftly your names change, these days! You threaten to confuse me, Duke Dorian!'

'You say my names change. You have known me in different guises?'

'Certainly. Enough for this particular conversation to have a boring familiarity.' Jhary-a-Conel grinned.

'Tell me some of those names.'

Jhary frowned. 'My memory is poor on such matters. Sometimes it seems to me I can recall a great deal of past (and future) incarnations. At other times, like this one, my mind refuses to consider anything but immediate problems.'

'I find that inconvenient,' said Hawkmoon. He looked up, as if he might see the bridge, but there was only mist. He prayed that Yisselda was safe, that she was still on her way to Londra.

'Oh, so do I, Duke Dorian. I wonder if I have any business here at all, you know.' Jhary-a-Conel pulled strongly at his oars.

'What of the "Conjunction of the Million Spheres"? Does your faulty memory serve you with any information concerning that phrase?'

Jhary-a-Conel frowned. 'It rings a distant bell. An event of some importance, I should have thought. Tell me more.'

'There is no more I can tell you. I had hoped . . .'

'If I should remember anything, I will tell you.'

The cat mewled again and Jhary craned his head around. 'Aha! Land of some sort. Let us hope it is friendly.'

'You have no idea where we are, then?'

'None at all, Duke Dorian.' The bottom of the boat scraped against shingle. 'Somewhere in one of the Fifteen Planes, it's to be hoped.'

4

THE GATHERING OF THE WISE

They had walked for five miles over chalky hills and seen no sign that this land was inhabited. Hawkmoon had told Jhary-a-Conel of everything that had befallen him, of everything which puzzled him. He remembered little of the adventure of Garathorm and Jhary remembered more, speaking of the Lords of Chaos, of Limbo and the perpetual struggle between the Gods, but all their conversation, as conversation often will, caused further confusion and at length they agreed to put an end to their various speculations.

'Only one thing I know, and I know that in my bones,' said Jhary-a-Conel, 'and that is that you need not fear for your Yisselda. I must admit that I am, by nature, optimistic – against considerable evidence on occasion – and I know that in this venture we stand to win much or lose all. That creature you encountered on the bridge must have considerable power if he could wrench you from your own world, and there is no question, of course, that he means you ill, but I have no inkling of his identity or when he will find us again. It seems to me that your ambition to find Tanelorn is pertinent.'

'Aye,' Hawkmoon looked around him. They stood on the crown of one of many low hills. The sky was clearing and the mist had vanished altogether and there was an eery silence and the landscape was remarkable in that all that seemed to live was the grass itself; there were no birds, no signs of the kind of wildlife which might be expected to flourish here in the absence of man. 'Yet our chances of finding Tanelorn seem singularly poor at this particular moment, Jhary-a-Conel.'

Jhary reached up to his shoulder to stroke the black and white cat which had sat there patiently since they had begun their march inland. 'I am bound to agree,' he said. 'Nonetheless it seems to me that our coming to this silent land was not merely fortuitous. We are bound to have friends, you know, as well as enemies.'

'Sometimes I doubt the worth of the kind of friends you mean,' Hawkmoon said bitterly, remembering Orland Fank and the Runestaff. 'Friends or enemies – we are still their pawns.'

'Well,' said Jhary-a-Conel with a grin, 'not pawns, perhaps – you must judge your worth better than that – why, I myself am at least a knight!'

'My objection,' said Hawkmoon firmly, 'is to being placed on the board at all.'

'Then it is for you to remove yourself from it,' Jhary said mysteriously, adding: 'Even if it should mean the destruction of the board itself.' He refused to amplify this remark, saying that it was intuition, not logic, which had led him to make it. But the remark had considerable resonance in Hawkmoon's mind and, oddly, it improved his spirits considerably. With increased energy, he set off again, taking such great strides that Jhary was hard put to keep up with him and soon began to complain, begging Hawkmoon to slow a little.

'We are not exactly certain where we are going, after all,' said Jhary.

Hawkmoon laughed. 'Indeed! But at this moment, Jhary-a-Conel, I care not if we head for Hell!'

The low hills rolled on in all directions and by nightfall their legs were aching greatly and their stomachs felt exceptionally empty and still there was no sign that this world was populated by any living thing but themselves.

'We should be grateful, I suppose,' said Hawkmoon, 'that the weather is reasonably clement.'

'Though dull,' added Jhary. 'Neither hot nor cold.

Could this be some pleasanter corner of Limbo, I wonder?'

Hawkmoon's attention was no longer with his friend. He was peering through the dusk. 'Look, Jhary. Yonder. Do you see something?'

Jhary followed Hawkmoon's pointing hand. He screwed up his eyes. 'On the brow of the hill?'

'Aye. Is it a man?'

'I think it is.' Impulsively, Jhary cupped his hands around his mouth, shouting: 'Hey! Can you see us? Are you a native of these parts, sir?'

Suddenly the figure was very much closer. It had an aura of black fire flickering around its whole body. It was clad in black, shining stuff that was not metal. Its dark face was hidden by a high collar, but enough was visible for Hawkmoon to recognize it.

'Sword . . .' said the figure. 'Me,' it said. 'Elric.'

'Who are you?' This was Jhary speaking. Hawkmoon could not speak – his throat was cramped, his lips dry. 'Is this your world.'

Fierce agony burned in the eyes; fierce hatred burned there. The figure made a motion towards Jhary – a belligerent motion as if he would tear the little man apart – but then something stopped him. He drew back. He looked at Hawkmoon again. He was snarling. 'Love,' he said. 'Love.' He spoke the word as if it was new to him, as if he were trying to learn it. The black flame around his body flared, flickered and dimmed, like a breeze-blown candle. He gasped. He pointed at Hawkmoon. He raised his other hand, as if to bar Hawkmoon's path. 'Do not go. We have been too long together. We cannot part. Once I commanded. Now I plead with you. What have I done for you but help you in all your many manifestations? Now they have taken my form away. You must find it, Elric. That is why you live again.'

'I am not Elric. I am Hawkmoon.'

'Ah, yes. I remember now. The jewel. The jewel will

do. But the sword is better.' The beautiful features writhed in pain. The horrid eyes glared, so filled with anguish that it was plain they could not see Hawkmoon at that moment. The fingers curled like hawk's claws. The body shuddered. The flame waned.

'Who are you?' said Hawkmoon this time.

'I have no name, unless you give me one. I have no form, unless you find it for me. I have only power. Ah! And pain!' The figure's features writhed again. 'I need . . . I need . . .'

Jhary made an impatient movement towards his hip, but Hawkmoon's hand stayed him. 'No. Do not draw it.'

'The sword,' said the creature eagerly.

'No,' said Hawkmoon quietly. And he did not know what he refused the creature. It was dark now, but the figure's darker aura pierced the ordinary blackness of the night.

'A sword!' It was a demand. A scream. 'A sword!'

For the first time, Hawkmoon realized that the creature had no weapons of its own. 'Find arms, if you wish them,' he said. 'You shall not have ours.'

Lightning leaped suddenly from the ground around the creature's feet. It gasped. It hissed. It shrieked. 'You will come to me! You will need me! Foolish Elric! Silly Hawkmoon! Stupid Erekosë! Pathetic Corum! You will need me!'

The scream seemed to last for several moments, even after the figure had vanished.

'It knows all your names,' said Jhary-a-Conel. 'Do you know what it is called?'

Hawkmoon shook his head. 'Not even in my dreams.'

'It is new to me,' Jhary told him. 'In all my many lives I do not think I have encountered it before. My memory is never good, at the best of times, but I would know if I had seen that being before. This is a strange adventure, an adventure of unusual significance.'

Hawkmoon interrupted his friend's musings. He pointed down into the valley. 'Would you say that was a fire, Jhary? A camp fire. Perhaps we are to meet the denizens of this world at long last.'

Without debating the wisdom of approaching the fire directly, they began to plod down the hill, coming at last to the floor of the valley. The fire was only a short distance from them now.

As they approached Hawkmoon saw that the fire was surrounded by a group of men, but what was peculiar about the scene was that each of the men was mounted on a horse and each horse faced inward, so that the group made a perfect, silent circle. So still were the horses, so stolidly did the riders sit in their saddles, that if it had not been for the sight of their breath steaming from their lips, Hawkmoon would have guessed them to be statues.

'Good evening,' he said boldly, but he received no reply from any of them. 'We are travellers who have lost our way and would appreciate your help in finding it again.'

The rider nearest to Hawkmoon turned his long head. 'It is why we are here, Sir Champion. It is why we have gathered. Welcome. We have been waiting for you.'

Now that Hawkmoon saw it closer to, he realized that the fire was no ordinary fire. Rather, it was a radiance, emanating from a sphere about the size of his fist. The sphere hovered a foot above the ground. Within it Hawkmoon thought he could see other spheres circulating. He returned his attention to the mounted men. He did not recognize the one who had spoken: a tall, black man, his body half naked, his shoulders swathed in a cloak of white fox fur. He made a short, polite bow. 'You have the advantage of me,' he said.

'You know me,' the black man told him, 'in at least one of your parallel existences. I'm named Sepiriz, the Last of the Ten.'

'And this is your world?'

Sepiriz shook his head. 'This is no one's world. This world still waits to be populated.' He looked beyond Hawkmoon at Jhary-a-Conel. 'Greetings, Master Moonglum of Elwher.'

'I am called Jhary-a-Conel at present,' Jhary told him.

'Yes,' said Sepiriz. 'Your face is different. And your body, now I look closely. Still, you did well in bringing the Champion to us.'

Hawkmoon glanced at Jhary. 'You knew where we were going?'

Jhary spread his hands. 'Only in the back of my mind. I could not have told you, if you had asked.' He stared frankly at the circle of horsemen. 'So you are all here.'

'You know them all?' asked Hawkmoon.

'I think so. My Lord Sepiriz – from the Chasm of Nihrain are you not? And Abaris, the Magi.' This an old man clad in a rich gown embroidered with curious symbols. He smiled a quiet smile, acknowledging his name. 'And you are Lamsar the Hermit,' said Jhary-a-Conel to the next horseman, who was even older than Abaris, and dressed in oiled leather to which patches of sand clung. His beard, too, had sand in it. 'I greet you,' he murmured.

In astonishment, Hawkmoon recognized another of the riders. 'You are dead,' he said. 'You died in defence of the Runestaff at Dnark.'

There came laughter from within the mysterious helm as the Warrior in Jet and Gold, Orland Fank's brother, flung back his armoured head. 'Some deaths are more permanent than others, Duke of Köln.'

'And you are Aleryon of the Temple of Law,' said Jhary to another old man, a pale, beardless man. 'Lord Arkyn's servant. And you are Amergin the Archdruid. I know you, too.'

Amergin, handsome, his hair bound with gold, his white garments loose on his lean body, inclined a grave head.

The last rider was a woman, her face completely covered by a golden veil, her filmy robes all of a kind of silver colour. 'Your name, lady, escapes me,' said Jhary, 'though I think I recognize you from some other world.'

And Hawkmoon found himself saying. 'You were slain on the Southern Ice. The Lady of the Chalice. The Silver Queen. Slain by . . .'

'By the Black Sword? Count Urlik, I would not have known you.' Her voice was sad and it was sweet and suddenly Hawkmoon saw himself, clad all in furs and armour, standing on a plain of glinting ice, a huge and horrible sword in his hand, and he shut his eyes tight and groaned. 'No . . .'

'It is over,' she said. 'It is over. I did you a great disservice, Sir Champion. Now I would help you further.'

The seven riders dismounted as one and moved closer to the small sphere.

'What is that globe?' asked Jhary-a-Conel nervously. 'It is magical, is it not.'

'It is what allows all seven of us to remain upon this plane,' said Sepiriz. 'We are, as you know, considered wise in our own worlds. This gathering was called so that we could debate events, for all of us has had the same experience. Our wisdom came from beings greater than ourselves. They gave us their knowledge when we called upon them for it. But, of late, it has been impossible to seek that knowledge. They are all engaged in matters of such moment that they have no time for us. To some of us these beings are known as the Lords of Law and we serve them as their messengers – in return they illuminate our minds. But we have had no word from those great Lords and we fear that they are under attack from a force greater than any they have previously encountered.'

'From Chaos?' Jhary asked.

'Possibly. But we have learned, too, that Chaos is under attack also, and not from Law. The Cosmic Balance itself, it seems, is threatened.'

'And that is why the Runestaff has been called from my world,' said Hawkmoon.

'That is why,' agreed the Warrior in Jet and Gold.

'And do you have any inkling of the nature of this threat?' Jhary asked.

'None, save that it seems to have something to do with the Conjunction of the Million Spheres. But you know of that, Sir Champion.' Sepiriz was about to continue when Jhary raised a hand to stop him.

'I know the phrase, but no more. My bad memory – which saves me from so much grief – tricks me again . . .'

'Ah,' said Sepiriz, frowning. 'Then perhaps we should not speak of it . . .'

'Speak of it, I beg you,' said Hawkmoon, 'for the phrase means much to me.'

'Law and Chaos are engaged in a great war – a war fought on all the planes of the Earth – a war in which humanity is completely, unwittingly, involved. You, as humanity's Champion, fight in each of your manifestations – ostensibly on the side of Law (though even that is disputed).' Sepiriz sighed. 'But Law and Chaos exhaust themselves. Some think they lose the power to maintain the Cosmic Balance and that when the Balance fades, then all existence ends. Others believe the Balance and the Gods all doomed, that the time of the Conjunction of the Million Spheres has come to us. I have said nothing of this to Elric, in my native world, for he is already greatly confused. I do not know how much to tell you, Hawkmoon. The morality of guessing at such monumental problems disturbs me. Yet if Elric is to blow the Horn of Fate –'

'And Corum to release Kwll,' added Aleryon.

'And Erekosë to come to Tanelorn,' said the Lady of the Chalice.

'– then it can only result in a cosmic disruption of

unimaginable magnitude. Our wisdom fails us. We are almost afraid to act; there is nothing to advise us. No one to tell us what the best course may be . . .'

'No one, save the Captain,' said Abaris of the Magi.

'And how do we know that he does not work for his own ends? How do we know if he is as altruistic as he makes out?' Lamsar the Hermit spoke in a tone of worried bewilderment. 'We know nothing of him. He has only recently appeared in the Fifteen Planes.'

'The Captain?' Hawkmoon said eagerly. 'Is he a being who radiates darkness?' He described the creature he had seen on the bridge and, earlier, in this world.

Sepiriz shook his head. 'That being some of us have seen briefly – but he, too, is mysterious. That is why we are so uncertain – these different creatures come to the multiverse and we know nothing of them. Our wisdom fails us . . .'

'Only the Captain has confidence,' said Amergin. 'He must go to him. We cannot help.' He looked intently at the shining globe in their midst. 'The little sphere – is the light fading?'

Hawkmoon looked at the sphere and saw that Amergin was right. 'Is that significant?' he asked.

'It means that we have little time left here,' said Sepiriz. 'We are to be recalled to our own worlds, our own times. We shall never be able to meet again in this way.'

'Tell me more of the Conjunction of the Million Spheres,' said Hawkmoon.

'Seek Tanelorn,' said the Lady of the Chalice.

'Avoid the Black Sword,' said Lamsar the Hermit.

'Go back to the ocean,' said the Warrior in Jet and Gold. 'Take passage on the Dark Ship.'

'And what of the Runestaff?' Hawkmoon said. 'Must I continue to serve that?'

'Only if it will serve you,' said the Warrior in Jet and Gold.

Now the light from the sphere was very dim and the seven were mounting their horses; they had become shadows.

'And my children,' Hawkmoon called. 'Where are they?'

'In Tanelorn,' said the Lady of the Chalice. 'They wait to be reborn.'

'Explain!' Hawkmoon pleaded. 'Lady – explain!'

But her shadow was the first to fade with the last of the light from the sphere. Soon only the black giant Sepiriz remained and his voice was very faint.

'I envy you your greatness, Champion Eternal, but I do not envy you your struggle.'

And into the blackness Hawkmoon shouted:

'It is not enough! It is not enough! I must know more!'

Jhary placed a sympathetic hand upon his arm. 'Come, Duke Dorian, we shall only learn more by doing as they instructed. Come, let us go back to the ocean.'

But then Jhary was gone and Hawkmoon was alone.

'Jhary-a-Conel? Jhary?'

Hawkmoon began to run through the night, to run through the silence, his mouth gaping to emit a scream which would not come, his eyes stinging with tears which would not flow, and in his ears he could hear nothing but his own heart beating like a funeral drum.

5

ON THE SHORE

And now it was dawn and the mist was on the sea, spilling aboard the stony land; and there were lights, silver-grey, drifting in the mist, and the cliffs behind Hawkmoon were ghastly. He had not slept. He felt a ghost in a ghost's world. He was abandoned, and still he had not wept. His eyes stared into the mist, his cold hands gripped the cold pommel of his sword, his white breath streamed from lips and nostrils, and he waited as a morning hunter awaits his prey, making no sound himself lest he fail to hear that betraying small noise which will reveal the object of his watch. Having no other possible action but to obey the advice of the seven wise ones who had spoken to him in the previous night, he waited for the ship which they had told him would come. He waited, uncaring if it came or not, but he knew that it would come.

Now a spot of red gleamed above his head and he thought at first it was the sun, but the tint was too deep, it was ruby coloured. Some star gleaming from an alien firmament, he thought. The red light tinged the mist, turning it pink. At the same time he heard a rhythmical creaking from the water and he knew that a ship was heaving-to. He heard an anchor fall, heard the murmur of voices, heard the rattle of a pulley and a bumping as of a small boat being lowered. He returned his attention to the red star, but it was gone, only its light was left. The mist parted. He saw a high ship in outline, its fore and aft decks considerably taller than the main deck; a lantern shone at prow and stern, rising and falling with the waves. The sails were furled, mast and rails were carved intricately, the style of the workmanship wholly unfamiliar.

'Please . . .'

Hawkmoon looked to his left and there stood the creature, its black aura dancing about it, its burning eyes entreating him.

'You irritate me, sir,' said Hawkmoon. 'I have no time for you.'

'Sword . . .'

'Find yourself a sword – then I'll be happy to fight you, if that is what you desire.' He spoke with a confidence of tone not matched by the fear which steadily grew in him. He refused to look at the figure.

'The ship . . .' said the creature. 'Me . . .'

'What?' Hawkmoon turned and saw that the eyes were leering at him now with full awareness of his state of mind.

'Let me come with you,' said the creature. 'I can help you there. You will need help.'

'Not yours,' said Hawkmoon, glancing at the water and seeing the boat which had been sent for him.

An armoured man stood upright in the boat. His armour had been fashioned to follow certain rules of geometry, rather than to serve in the practical business of protection against an enemy's weapons. His great, beaked helmet hid much of his face, but bright, blue eyes were evident, and a curling, golden beard.

'Sir Hawkmoon?' The armoured man's voice was light, friendly. 'I am Brut, a knight of Lashmar. I believe we are engaged upon a common quest.'

'A quest?' Hawkmoon noticed that the dark figure had disappeared.

'For Tanelorn?'

'Aye. I seek Tanelorn.'

'Then you will find allies aboard the ship.'

'What is the ship? Where is it bound?'

'Only those who sail with her know that.'

'Is there one called "Captain" aboard?'

'Aye, our Captain. He is aboard.' Brut climbed from the

boat and held it against the movement of the waves. Those who rowed turned their heads to look at Hawkmoon. They were all experienced faces, the faces of men who had fought in more than a single battle. Warrior Hawkmoon knew other warriors when he saw them.

'And who are these?'

'Comrades of ours.'

'What makes us comrades?'

'Why?' Brut smiled with good humour belying the import of his words. 'We are all damned, sir.'

For some reason this statement relieved rather than disturbed Hawkmoon. He laughed, striding forward, letting Brut help him into the boat. 'Do any but the damned seek for Tanelorn?'

'I have never heard of any others.' Brut clapped a hand on Hawkmoon's shoulder as he joined him. The boat was seized by the waves and the warriors bent their backs again, turning round and rowing for where the ship awaited them, its dark, polished timbers still catching a little of the ruby coloured light from above. Hawkmoon admired its lines, admired its high, curved prow.

'It is a ship belonging to no fleet I've ever seen,' he said.

'It belongs to no fleet at all, Sir Hawkmoon.'

Hawkmoon looked back, but the land had vanished. Only familiar mist was there.

'How came you to that shore?' Brut asked him.

'You know not? I thought you would. I had hoped for answers to my questions. I was told to wait for the ship there. I became lost – thrown from my own world and the ones I love by a creature which hates me and professes to love me.'

'A god?'

'A god without the usual qualities, if he be a god,' Hawkmoon said dryly.

'I have heard that the gods are losing their most impressive qualities,' said Brut of Lashmar. 'Their powers are stretched so thin.'

'In this world?'

'This is no "world",' said Brut, almost in surprise.

The boat reached the ship and Hawkmoon saw that a stout ladder had been uncurled in readiness for them. Brut held the bottom for him, signing for him to climb. Quelling his caution, which desired him to consider his actions before going aboard the ship, Hawkmoon began to ascend.

There came a cry from above. Davits were swung out to take the boat up. A wave caught the ship and it swayed, moaning. Hawkmoon climbed slowly. He heard the crack of an unfurling sail, he heard a creak as a capstan turned. He raised his eyes, but they were blinded by a sudden beam from the red star overhead, which was again revealed by a rent in the clouds.

'That star,' he called. 'What is it, Brut of Lashmar? Do you follow it?'

'No,' said the blond soldier. His voice was suddenly bleak. 'It follows us.'

BOOK TWO

SAILING BETWEEN THE WORLDS:
SAILING FOR TANELORN . . .

1

THE WAITING WARRIORS

Hawkmoon looked about him while Brut of Lashmar joined him on deck. Already a wind had sprung up and was filling the great, black sail. It was a familiar wind. Hawkmoon had experienced it at least once before, when he and Count Brass had fought Kalan, Taragorm and their minions in the caverns below Londra, when the very essence of Time and Space had been disrupted thanks to the efforts of the Dark Empire's two greatest sorcerer scientists. But, for all that it was a familiar wind, Hawkmoon did not care to feel its breath upon his flesh and he was grateful when Brut escorted him along the deck and flung open the door of the stern cabin. Heat poured out, welcoming him. A big lantern swayed here, hanging from four silver chains, its light spreading through the relatively large space, diffused by red-grey glass. In the centre of the cabin stood a heavy sea-table, its legs firmly clamped to the boards. A number of big, carved chairs were fixed around this table and some of the chairs were occupied, while elsewhere men stood up. All looked curiously at Hawkmoon as he entered.

'This is Dorian Hawkmoon, Duke of Köln,' said Brut. 'I'll rejoin my fellows in my own cabin. I'll call for you again soon, Sir Hawkmoon, for we'll need to pay our respects to the Captain.'

'Does he know who I am? Does he know I'm aboard?'

'Of course. He selects a crew carefully, does the Captain.' Brut laughed and his laughter was echoed by the grim, hard men in the cabin.

Hawkmoon's attention was drawn to one of the standing men – a warrior with unusual features, wearing armour of such delicate workmanship that it had an almost ethereal quality to it. Over his right eye was a brocaded patch and on his left hand a glove of what Hawkmoon guessed to be silvered steel (except he knew in his heart that it was not). The warrior's pointed face and slanting, slender brows, his eye which was purple, with a pupil of soft yellow and his filmy, pale hair, all spoke of his membership of a race only slightly related to Hawkmoon's. Yet Hawkmoon felt a kinship with him that was strong, that was magnetic (and that was frightening, too).

'I am Prince Corum of the Scarlet Robe,' said the warrior, striding forward. 'You are Hawkmoon, are you not, of the Runestaff?'

'You know of me?'

'I have seen you, often. In visions, sir – in dreams. Do you not know me?'

'No . . .' But Hawkmoon did know Prince Corum. He had seen him, too, in visions. 'I admit that – yes, I do know you . . .'

Prince Corum smiled a sad, grim smile.

'How long have you been aboard this ship?' Hawkmoon asked him, sitting down in one of the chairs and accepting a goblet of wine offered him by one of the other warriors.

'Who knows?' said Corum. 'A day or a century. It is a dream ship. I boarded it thinking I would reach the past. The last I remember of any event before boarding was being slain – betrayed by one I thought I loved. Then I was on a misty shore, convinced that my soul had gone to Limbo, and this ship hailed me. Having nought else to do, I joined it. Since then others have filled the berths here. There is one left, I am told, then we have a full complement. I gather we sail now to pick up this last passenger.'

'And our destination?'

Corum took a draught from his own wine cup. 'I have heard the name Tanelorn spoken, but the Captain told me nothing of that. Perhaps the name is spoken in hope. I have received no evidence of any specific destination.'

'Then Brut of Lashmar was deceiving me.'

'Deceiving himself, more like,' said Corum. 'But perhaps Tanelorn is where we are bound. I have been there once, I seem to remember.'

'And did you find peace there?'

'Briefly, sir, I think.'

'Your memory, then, is poor?'

'It is no worse than the memories of most of us who sail on the Dark Ship,' said Corum.

'Have you heard of the Conjunction of the Million Spheres?'

'Yes, it strikes a chord. A time of great changes, is it not, on all the planes? When the planes intersect at specific points in their histories. When our normal perception of Time and of Space becomes meaningless and when it is possible for radical alterations to be made in the nature of reality itself. When old gods die . . .'

'And new ones are born?'

'Perhaps. If they are needed.'

'You can amplify, sir?'

'If my memory were jogged, Dorian Hawkmoon, I am sure that I could. There is much in my head which will not, as it were, come forward. Knowledge is there, but also pain – and perhaps the pain and the knowledge are too closely linked, so that one is buried with the other. I believe I have been mad.'

'I, too,' said Hawkmoon. 'But I have been sane, also. Now I'm neither. It is an odd feeling.'

'I know it well, sir.' Corum turned, indicating the other occupants of the cabin with his cup. 'You must meet your comrades. This is Emshon of Ariso . . .' A fierce-faced little man with heavy moustaches and a glowering manner looked up from the table, grunting at Hawkmoon. He had a thin tube in his hand which he lifted frequently to his

lips. Within the tube were herbs of some kind, smouldering, and it was their smoke which the dwarfish warrior
inhaled. 'Greetings, Hawkmoon,' he said. 'I hope you're a
better sailor than myself, for this damned ship's inclined to
pitch like an unwilling virgin at times.'

'Emshon has a gloomy disposition,' said Corum smiling,
'and something of a coarse manner of speech, but he's
agreeable enough company most of the time. And this is
Keeth Woecarrier, who is convinced he brings doom to all
he rides with . . .'

Keeth looked shyly away, muttering something which
none could hear. From beneath his bearskin cloak he
raised a huge hand in greeting, and all that Hawkmoon
heard of his words was: 'It's true. It's true.' He was a big,
lumbering soldier, dressed in patched leather and wool,
with a skin cap upon his head.

'John ap-Rhyss.' This was a tall, thin man with hair
falling well below his shoulders and a drooping moustache
adding to his melancholy look, clad all in faded black, save
for a bright insignia stitched to his shirt above his heart.
He wore a dark wide-brimmed hat and his grin of greeting
was sardonic. 'Hail to you, Duke Dorian. We have heard
of your exploits in the land of Yel. You fight the Dark
Empire, do you not?'

'I did,' said Hawkmoon. 'But that fight is now won.'

'Have I been away so long?' John ap-Rhyss frowned.

'It is useless to measure Time in the ordinary way,'
Corum said warningly. 'Accept that in Hawkmoon's
immediate past the Dark Empire is defeated – in yours, it
is still strong.'

'I am called Turning Nikhe,' said the one closest to John
ap-Rhyss. He was bearded, red-haired, with a quiet, wry
manner. In contrast to ap-Rhyss, he was covered all over
in jingling talismans, in beads, decorated leather,
embroidery, charms of gold, silver and brass. His sword-
belt was embedded with semi-precious jewels, with little

falcons of bronze, with stars and arrows. 'I have my name because I once changed sides during a battle, and am considered a traitor in certain parts of my own world (though I had my reasons for doing what I did). Be warned of that, however. I am not a land soldier, as most of you, but a sailor. My own ship was rammed by ships of King Fesfaton's navy. I was drowning when rescued by this vessel. I had thought I'd be needed for crew, but find myself a passenger.'

'Who crews the ship, then?' Hawkmoon asked, for he had seen none but these warriors.

Turning Nikhe laughed in his red beard. 'Forgive me,' he said. 'But there are no sailors aboard, save you count the Captain.'

'The ships sails herself,' said Corum quietly. 'And we have speculated on whether she is commanded by the Captain or whether she commands him.'

'It's a sorcerous ship and I wish I had no part of her,' said one who had not yet spoken. He was fat, sporting a steel breastplate engraved with naked women in all manner of poses. Beneath this he wore a red silk shirt and there was a black neckerchief at his throat. He had golden rings in the lobes of his large ears and his black hair fell in ringlets to his shoulders. His black beard was trimmed and tapered and his moustache curled over his swarthy cheeks, almost to his hard, brown eyes. 'I am Baron Gotterin of Nimplaset-in-Khorg and I know where this ship is bound.'

'Where, sir?'

'For Hell, sir. I am dead, as we all are – though some are too cowardly to admit it. On Earth I sinned with zest and with imagination and am in no doubt of my fate.'

'Your imagination fails you now, Baron Gotterin,' said Corum dryly. 'You take a view which is exceptionally conventional.'

Baron Gotterin shrugged his big shoulders and took a deep interest in the contents of his wine cup.

An old man stepped out of the shadows. He was thin, but strong, and he wore garments of stained, yellow leather which accentuated his pallor. On his head was a dented battle cap, of wood and iron, the wood studded with brass nails. His eyes were bloodshot, moody and his mouth had a morose set to it. He scratched the back of his neck, saying: 'I'd rather be in Hell than imprisoned here. I'm a soldier, as we all are, and keen to be at my trade. I am most dreadfully bored.' He nodded to Hawkmoon. 'I'm called Chaz of Elaquol and I have the distinction of never having served in a victorious army. I was fleeing, defeated as usual, when I was driven by my pursuers into the sea. My luck is useless in battle, but I have never been captured. This, however, was the strangest rescue of them all!'

'Thereod of the Caves,' said one even paler than Chaz, presenting himself. 'I greet you, Hawkmoon. This is my first voyage, so I find all its aspects interesting.' He was the youngest of the company, with an awkward manner of moving. He wore the faintly scintillating skins of some reptile and there was a cap on his head of the same stuff, and he had a sword so long that it jutted a foot above his back (on which it was slung) and almost touched the floor.

The last to be introduced had to be shaken awake by Corum. He sat at the far end of the table, an empty goblet still in his gloved hand, his face hidden by the fair hair hanging over it. He belched, grinned apologetically, looked at Hawkmoon with friendly, foolish eyes, poured himself more wine, drank off the whole goblet, made to speak, failed, and closed his eyes again. He began to snore.

'That's Reingir,' said Corum, 'nicknamed "The Rock", though how he came by the name he has never been sober enough to tell us! He was drunk when he came aboard and has kept himself in that state ever since, though he's amiable enough and sometimes sings for us.'

'And you know not why we have all been gathered?'

Hawkmoon asked. 'We are all soldiers, but appear to have little else in common.'

'We have been picked to fight some enemy of the Captain's,' said Emshon. 'All I know is that it's not *my* fight and I would have preferred to have been consulted before being selected. I had a plan to storm the Captain's cabin and take over the ship, sailing for pleasanter climes than these (have you noticed it is always misty?) but these "heroes" would have none of it. You've precious little in the way of guts. The Captain would only have to fart and you'd scatter!'

The others took this with amusement. Evidently, they were used to Emshon's *braggadocio*.

'Do you know why we're here, Prince Corum?' Hawkmoon asked. 'Have you spoken with the Captain?'

'Aye – spoken at some length. But I'll say nothing until you've seen him.'

'And when will that be?'

'Quite soon, I'd think. Each of us has been summoned shortly after coming aboard.'

'And told next to nothing!' complained Chaz of Elaquol. 'All I want to know is when the fight begins. And I pray that it's won. I'd like to be on a winning side before I die!'

John ap-Rhyss smiled, showing his teeth. 'You do not instil us with confidence, Sir Chaz, with your many tales of defeat.'

Chaz said seriously. 'I care not if I survive the coming battle or not, but I have a feeling in my bones that it will be successful for some of us.'

'Only some?' Emshon of Ariso snorted and made a bad-tempered gesture. 'Successful for the Captain, maybe.'

'I am inclined to think that we are privileged,' said Turning Nikhe quietly. 'There is not one of us here who was not close to death before the Dark Ship found us. If we are to die, then it will probably be in some great cause.'

'You are a romantic, sir,' said Baron Gotterin. 'I am a

realist. I believe nothing of what the Captain has told us. I know for certain that we go to our punishments.'

'Everything you say, sir, proves only one thing – that you possess a dull and primitive conscience!' Emshon was plainly pleased with his own remark. He smirked.

Baron Gotterin turned away and found himself staring into the melancholy eye of Keeth Woecarrier who made an embarrassed noise and looked at the floor.

'This bickering frets me,' said Thereod of the Caves. 'Will anyone join me in a game of chess?' He indicated a large board fastened by leather straps to a bulwark.

'I'll play,' said Emshon, 'though I tire of beating you.'

'The game is new to me,' said Thereod mildly. 'But I learn, Emshon, that you'll admit.'

Emshon rose from the table and helped Thereod unstrap the board. Together they carried it to the table and clipped it into place. From a chest Thereod took out a box of pieces and began to arrange them. Some of the others gathered to watch the game.

Hawkmoon addressed Corum. 'Are all of these counterparts of ourselves?'

'Counterparts or other incarnations, do you mean?'

'Other manifestations of the so-called Champion Eternal,' said Hawkmoon. 'Do you know the theory. It explains why we recognize each other, why we have seen each other in visions.'

'I know the theory well,' said Corum. 'But I do not believe most of these warriors are our counterparts, as you call them. Some, like John ap-Rhyss, are from the same worlds. No, in this company, I think only you and I share – what? – a soul?'

Hawkmoon looked hard at Corum. And then he shivered.

52

2

THE BLIND CAPTAIN

Hawkmoon had no idea how much time had passed before Brut came back to the cabin, but Emshon and Thereod had played two games of chess and were half-way through another.

'The Captain is ready to receive you, Hawkmoon.' Brut looked tired; mist streamed in through the open door before he could slam it shut.

Hawkmoon got up from his chair. His sword caught under the table and he freed it so that it swung to its usual position on his thigh. He drew his cloak about him, fastening the clasp.

'Don't spring so readily to his bidding,' Emshon said grumpily, raising his eyes from the board. 'He needs us, does the Captain, for whatever his venture is.'

Hawkmoon smiled. 'I must satisfy my curiosity. Emshon of Ariso.'

He followed Brut from the cabin and along the chilly deck. He thought that he had noticed a large wheel forward, when he boarded, and now he saw one at the stern. He commented on this to Brut.

Brut nodded. 'There are two. But only one steersman. Apart from the Captain, he seems to have been the only other being on board.' Brut pointed through the thick, white mist, and there was the outline of a man, his two hands upon the wheel. He stood extraordinarily still, dressed in thick, quilted jerkin and leggings. He seemed fixed to the wheel, fixed to the deck, and Hawkmoon could have found himself doubting if the man lived at all . . . He could tell from the motion of the ship that she sailed with more than natural speed and, looking up at the sail, he saw that it was full, but no wind blew now, not even that unearthly wind with which he had become familiar. They passed a cabin identical to that which they had left and then reached the high forward deck. Under this was a door whose substance was not the same as the dark wood of the rest of the ship. It was of metal, but a metal which had a vibrant, organic quality to it, a russet cast which reminded Hawkmoon of the pelt of a fox.

'This is the Captain's cabin,' said Brut. 'I'll leave you here, Hawkmoon. I hope you receive answers to at least some of your questions.'

Brut walked back to his own cabin, leaving Hawkmoon contemplating the strange door. He stretched out a hand to touch the metal. It was warm. It sent a shock through him.

'Enter, Hawkmoon,' said a voice from within. It was a richly timbred voice, but it sounded remote.

Hawkmoon looked for a handle, but found none. He began to press on the door, but already it was opening. Bright, ruby light struck eyes grown used to the dimness of the stern cabin. Hawkmoon blinked, but moved towards the light, while the door closed behind him. The air was warm and sweetly scented; brass and gold and silver fixtures glinted; glass shone. Hawkmoon saw rich hangings, a deep, many-hued carpet, red lamps fixed to bulkheads, subtle carvings; there were purples, dark reds, dark greens and yellows; there was a polished desk, its rails of gleaming, twisted gold, and on the desk were instruments, charts, a book. There were chests, a curtained bunk. Beside the desk stood a tall man who might, in face and figure, have been a relative of Corum's. He had the same tapering head, the fine red-gold hair, the almond, slanting eyes. His loose garments were all of the same shade of buff and the sandals on his feet were of silver, while silver laces were wound about his calves. On his head was a circlet of blue jade. But it was the eyes which drew Hawkmoon's attention. They were a milky white, flecked with blue, and they were blind. The Captain smiled.

'Greetings, Hawkmoon. Have you been given our wine, yet?'

'I had some wine, aye.' Hawkmoon watched as the man moved deftly towards a chest on which were set out a silver jug and silver cups.

'You will have some more?'

'I thank you, sir.'

The Captain poured the wine and Hawkmoon picked up his cup. He sipped and the wine filled him with a sense of well-being. 'I have not had this vintage,' he said.

'It will restore you,' said the Captain, taking a cup for himself. 'And will have no ill-effects, I assure you.'

'There is a rumour on board, sir, that your ship is bound for Tanelorn.'

'There are many who sail with us who yearn for Tanelorn,' said the Captain, turning his blind head to face Hawkmoon. For a moment Hawkmoon thought that the Captain looked not at his face but directly into his soul. He crossed the cabin to one of the portholes and looked out at the white, swirling mist. The steady rising and falling forward motion of the ship seemed to become more pronounced.

'You answer cryptically,' said Hawkmoon. 'I had hoped that you would be more direct with me.'

'I am as direct as I can be, Duke Dorian, be assured of that.'

'Assurances . . .' began Hawkmoon, then held back the rest of the sentence.

'I know,' said the Captain. 'They are of little use to a mind in the torment which you must feel. But I believe that my ship takes you closer to Tanelorn and to your children.'

'You know that I seek my children?'

'Yes. I know that you are a victim of the disruptions

which have come about as a result of the Conjunction of the Million Spheres.'

'Can you tell me more of that, sir?'

'You know already that there are many worlds which exist in relation to your own, but separated by barriers which cut them off from your perception? You know that their histories are often similar, that the beings sometimes called the Lords of Law and the Lords of Chaos war permanently for domination of those worlds and that certain men and women have a destiny which involves them in those wars?'

'You speak of the Eternal Champion?'

'Of him and of those who share his fate.'

'Jhary-a-Conel?'

'That is one of his names. And Yisselda is another name. She has many counterparts, too.'

'And what of the Cosmic Balance?'

'Of the Cosmic Balance and the Runestaff little is known.'

'You do not serve either?'

'I do not believe so.'

'That, at least, is a relief to my ears,' said Hawkmoon, replacing his finished cup upon the chest. 'I have become tired of talk of great destinies.'

'I will speak of nothing but the practical business of survival,' the Captain told him. 'My ship has always sailed *between* the worlds – guarding, perhaps, the many borders where they are weakest. We have known no other life, I think, my steersman and I. I envy you that, Sir Champion – I envy you the variety of your experience.'

'I have a mind to exchange destinies, if you would like to, Captain.'

The blind man laughed quietly. 'I do not think that that is possible.'

'So my being aboard your ship has something to do with the Conjunction of the Million Spheres?'

'Everything. As you are aware, the event itself is rare enough. And this time the Lords of Law and Chaos and their many minions battle with particular ferocity to see which of them shall control the worlds when the Conjunction is passed. They involve yourself in all your guises, for you are important to them, make no mistake of that. As Corum, you have created a special problem for them.'

'Corum and I are the same, then?'

'Different manifestations of the same Hero, drawn from different worlds at different times. A dangerous business – normally two aspects of the Champion coexisting in the same world at the same time would be an alarming prospect – and we have four such aspects to consider. You have not yet met Erekosë?'

'No.'

'He inhabits the forward cabin. Eight other warriors are there, too. They await only Elric. We sail now to find him. He must be drawn from what would be your past, just as Corum has been drawn from what would be your future if you shared the same world. Such are the forces at work which make us risk monumental stakes! I pray that it will prove worthwhile.'

'And what are the forces at work?'

'I tell you what I have told the other two and what I will tell Elric. I can tell you no more, so ask no further questions when I have finished. Do you agree to that?'

'I must,' said Hawkmoon simply.

'When the time comes,' said the Captain, 'I will tell you all that there is left.'

'Continue, sir,' said Hawkmoon politely.

'Our destination is an island – a rare thing, for it is an island indigenous to these waters – inhabiting what you would call Limbo and, at the same time, inhabiting all the worlds on which mankind struggles. That island – or rather the city which stands upon the island – has been attacked many times and both Law and Chaos would control it, yet none has ever succeeded. Once it had the blessing of a people known as the Grey Lords, but they have since disappeared – none knows where. In their place have come enemies of immense power – beings who would destroy all the worlds forever. It is the Conjunction which has allowed them to enter this "multiverse" of ours. And having entered, having gained this foothold on our borders, they will not leave until they have effectively killed everything living.'

'They must be powerful indeed. And this ship has been called to gather a band of warriors to join forces with those who fight that enemy?'

'The ship goes to fight the enemy, yes.'

'But we must perish, surely?'

'No. Individually you in any one of your aspects would not have the power to destroy this enemy. That is why the others have been called. Later, I will tell you more.' The Captain paused, as if listening to something in the waters surrounding the ship. 'There! I think we are ready to find our last passenger. Go now, Hawkmoon. Forgive my manner, but you must leave me.'

'When will I learn more, sir?'

'Soon.' The Captain gestured at the door, which had opened. 'Soon.'

His head full of the information the Captain had given him, Hawkmoon stumbled back into the mist.

Far away, he could just hear the booming of surf, and he knew that the ship neared land. For a moment he thought he would remain on deck and view that land if he could, but then something made him change his mind and he hurried towards the stern cabin, casting a last look back at the rigid, mysterious figure of the steersman who was still at the forward wheel.

3

THE ISLAND OF SHADOWS

'And did the Captain illuminate you, Sir Hawkmoon?' Emshon fingered his chess queen as Hawkmoon entered the cabin.

'A little,' said Hawkmoon, 'though he mystified me more. Why do our numbers seem significant? Ten men to a cabin?'

'Is it not the maximum the cabins can hold comfortably?' asked Thereod, who seemed to be winning the game.

'There must be a considerable amount of space below,' Corum said. 'That cannot be the reason.'

'And what of sleeping quarters?' said Hawkmoon. 'You have been aboard longer than I. Where do you sleep?'

'We do not sleep,' said Baron Gotterin. The fat soldier jerked a thumb at the snoring Reingir. 'Save for that one. And he sleeps all the time.' He fingered his oiled beard. 'Who sleeps in Hell?'

'You have sung the same toneless song since you came aboard,' John ap-Rhyss said. 'A more polite man would be silent or find some new song to sing.'

Gotterin sneered and turned his back on his critic.

The tall, long-haired man from Yel sighed and resumed his drinking.

'The last of us is due to board soon, I gather,' said Hawkmoon. He looked at Corum. 'One named Elric. Is the name familiar?'

'It is. Is it not familiar to you?'

'It is.'

'Elric, Erekosë and myself fought together once, at a time of great crisis. The Runestaff saved us, then, at the fight at the Tower of Voilodion Ghagnasdiak.'

'What do you know of the Runestaff? Has it aught to do with the Cosmic Balance of which I have heard so much of late?'

'Possibly,' said Corum, 'but do not look to me for understanding of such mysteries, friend Hawkmoon. I am as bewildered as yourself.'

'Both seem to stand for Equilibrium.'

'True.'

'And yet I learn that the equilibrium is one maintaining the power of the gods. Why do we fight to maintain their power?'

Corum smiled reminiscently. 'Do we?' he said.

'Do we not?'

'Usually, I suppose,' said Corum.

'You become as irritating as the Captain,' said Hawkmoon with a laugh. 'What do you mean?'

Corum shook his head. 'I am not sure.'

Hawkmoon realized that he felt better than he had done for some while. He commented on this.

'You have drunk the Captain's wine,' said Corum. 'It is what sustains us, I think. There is more here. I offered you only the ordinary stuff, but if you desire . . .'

'Not now. But it sharpens the brain – it sharpens the brain.'

'Does it?' said Keeth Woecarrier from the shadows. 'I fear it dulls mine. I am confused.'

'We are all confused,' said Chaz of Elaquol dismissively. 'Who would not be?' He half drew his sword and then plunged it back into the scabbard. 'I am only clear-headed when I fight.'

'I gather that we shall be fighting soon,' Hawkmoon told him.

This drew the interest of them all and Hawkmoon repeated the little the Captain had said. The warriors fell, again, to speculating, and even Baron Gotterin brightened, speaking no more of Hell and punishment.

Hawkmoon had an inclination to avoid Prince Corum's company, not because he disliked the man (he found him most likeable) but because he was disturbed by the idea that he shared the cabin with one who was another incarnation of himself. Corum seemed to have a common feeling.

And so the time passed.

Later, the door of the cabin opened and two tall men stood there. One was of a darkish countenance, heavy and broad-shouldered, with many scars upon his face which was, though careworn, strikingly handsome. It was hard to tell his age, though he was probably close to forty, and his dark hair had a little silver in it. His deep-set eyes were intelligent, revealing something of a private grief. He was dressed in thick leather strengthened at the shoulders, elbows and wrists with steel plates which were much dented and scraped. He recognized Hawkmoon and nodded to Corum as if they had already met. His companion was slim and physically had much in common with Corum and the Captain. His eyes were crimson, smouldering like the coals of some supernatural fire, and they stared from a face which was bone-white, bloodless – the face of a corpse. His long hair, too, was white. His body was swathed in a heavy leather cloak, the hood thrown back. From under the cloak jutted the outlines of a great broadsword and Hawkmoon wondered why he should feel a frisson of fear when he observed that outline.

Corum recognized the albino. 'Elric of Melniboné! My theories become more meaningful!' He glanced eagerly at Hawkmoon, but Hawkmoon hung back, not sure that he welcomed the white swordsman. 'See, Hawkmoon, this is the one of whom I spoke.'

The albino was surprised, baffled. 'You know me, sir?'

Corum was smiling. 'You recognize me, Elric. You

61

must! At the Tower of Voilodion Ghagnasdiak? With Erekosë – though a different Erekosë.'

'I know of no such tower, no name which resembles that, and this is the first I have seen of Erekosë.' Elric looked to his companion, Erekosë, as if seeking help. 'You know me and you know my name, but I do not know you. I find this disconcerting, sir.'

The other spoke for the first time, his voice deep and vibrant and melancholy. 'I, too, had never met Prince Corum before he came aboard,' said Erekosë, 'yet he insists we fought together once. I am inclined to believe him. Time on the different planes does not always run concurrently. Prince Corum might well exist in what we would term the future.'

Hawkmoon found that his brain was refusing to hear any more. He longed for the relative simplicity of his own world. 'I had thought to find some relief from such paradoxes here,' he said. He rubbed at his eyes and his forehead, fingering, for an instant, the scar where the Black Jewel had once been imbedded. 'But it seems there is none at this present moment in the history of the planes. Everything is in flux and even our identities, it seems, are prone to alter at any moment.'

Corum was insistent, still addressing Elric. 'We were Three! Do you not recall it, Elric? The Three Who Are One?'

Evidently Elric knew nothing of which Corum spoke.

'Well,' said Corum with a shrug, 'now we are Four. Did the Captain say anything of an island we are supposed to invade?'

'He did.' The newcomer looked from face to face. 'Do you know who these enemies might be?'

Hawkmoon had a fellow feeling for the albino, then. 'We know no more or less than you do, Elric. I seek a place called Tanelorn and two children. Perhaps I seek the Runestaff, too. Of that I am not entirely sure.'

Corum, still eager to jog Elric's memory, said: 'We found it once. We three. In the Tower of Voilodion Ghagnasdiak. It was of considerable help to us.'

Hawkmoon wondered if Corum were mad. 'As it might be to me,' he said. 'I served it once. I gave it a great deal.' He stared hard at Elric, for the white face was becoming more familiar with every passing moment. He realized that he did not fear Elric. It was the sword which the albino bore – there was what Hawkmoon feared.

'We have much in common, as I told you, Elric.' Erekosë was plainly trying to remove the tensions from the atmosphere. 'Perhaps we share masters in common, too?'

Elric made something of an arrogant shrug. 'I serve no master but myself.'

Hawkmoon found himself smiling at this. The other two also smiled.

And when Erekosë murmured: 'On such ventures as these one is inclined to forget much, as one forgets a dream,' Hawkmoon found himself saying, with considerable conviction: 'This *is* a dream. Of late I've dreamt many such.'

And Corum, now acting as mediator himself, said: 'It is all dreaming, if you like. All existence.'

Elric made a dismissive gesture which Hawkmoon found a trifle irritating. 'Dream or reality, the experience amounts to the same, does it not?'

Erekosë's smile was soulful. 'Quite right.'

'In my own world,' said Hawkmoon sharply, 'we had a clear idea of the difference between dream and reality. Does not such vagueness produce a peculiar form of mental lethargy in us?'

'Can we afford to think?' Erekosë asked, almost savagely. 'Can we afford to analyse too closely? Can you, Sir Hawkmoon?'

And Hawkmoon knew, suddenly, what Erekosë's doom was. He knew that it was his doom, too. And he fell silent, shamed.

'I remember,' said Erekosë, more softly now. 'I was, am, or will be Dorian Hawkmoon. I remember.'

'And that is your grotesque and terrifying fate,' said Corum. 'We all share the same identity – but only you, Erekosë, remember them all.'

'I wish my memory were not so sharp,' said the heavy man. 'For so long have I sought Tanelorn and my Ermizhad. And now comes the Conjunction of the Million Spheres, when all the worlds intersect and there are pathways between them. If I can find the right path, then I shall see Ermizhad again. I shall see all that I hold dearest. And the Eternal Champion will rest. We shall all rest, for our fates are so closely linked together. The time has come again for me. This, I now know, is the second Conjunction I shall witness. The first wrenched me from a world and set me to warring. If I fail to take advantage of the second, I shall never know peace. This is my only opportunity. I pray that we do sail for Tanelorn.'

'I pray with you,' said Hawkmoon.

'So you should,' said Erekosë. 'So you should, sir.'

When the other two had gone, Hawkmoon agreed to join Corum in a game of chess (though he was still reluctant to spend much time in the other's company), but the game became strange – each able to anticipate exactly what his opponent would do. Corum took the experience with apparent lightness. Laughing, he sat back in his chair. 'There is little point to continuing, eh?'

Hawkmoon agreed with relief and, with relief, saw the door open and Brut of Lashmar entered, a jug of hot wine in one gloved hand.

'I bring the compliments of the Captain,' he said, placing the jug in an indentation at the centre of the table. 'Did you sleep well?'

'Sleep?' Hawkmoon was surprised. 'Have you slept?

Where do you sleep?'

Brut frowned. 'You were not informed, then, of the bunks below. How have you remained awake so long?'

Corum said hastily: 'Let us not pursue the question.'

'Drink the wine,' said Brut quietly. 'It will revive you.'

'Revive us?' Hawkmoon felt a wildness, a bitterness, rise in him. 'Or make us share the same dream?'

Corum poured wine for both of them and almost forced the cup into Hawkmoon's hand. He looked alarmed.

Hawkmoon made to dash the wine away, but Corum put his silver hand on Hawkmoon's arm. 'No, Hawkmoon. Drink. If the wine makes the dream coherent to all of us, then it is better.'

Hawkmoon hesitated, thought for an instant, disliked the drift of his thoughts, and he drank. The wine was good. It had the same influence as that which he had drunk in the Captain's company. His spirits improved. 'You are right,' he said to Corum.

'The Captain would have the Four join him now,' said Brut soberly.

'Has he more information for us?' Hawkmoon asked, aware that the other warriors in the cabin listened eagerly. One by one they came up to the wine jug and helped themselves from it. They drank as he had drunk, quickly.

Hawkmoon and Corum rose and followed Brut from the cabin. Walking along the deck, through the mist, Hawkmoon tried to see beyond the rail, but saw only mist. Then he noticed a man standing at the rail, his attitude introspective. He recognized Elric and called out in a friendlier tone than he had used before:

'The Captain has requested that we Four visit him in his cabin.'

Hawkmoon saw Erekosë leave his cabin, nodding to them. Elric left the rail and led the way up the deck to the forward deck and the red-brown door. He knocked; they entered the warmth and luxury of the cabin.

And the Captain's blind face greeted them, and he made a sign towards the chest, where the silver jug and the silver wine cups were, and he said:

'Please help yourselves, my friends.'

Hawkmoon found now that he was eager to drink, as were his companions.

'We are nearing our destination,' said the Captain. 'It will not be long before we disembark. I do not believe our enemies expect us, yet it will be a hard fight against those two.'

Hawkmoon had received the impression that they fought many. 'Two? Only two?'

'Only two.'

Hawkmoon glanced at the others, but they did not meet his gaze. They were looking at the Captain.

'A brother and a sister,' said the blind man. 'Sorcerers from quite another universe than ours. Due to recent disruptions in the fabric of our worlds – of which you know something, Hawkmoon, and you, too, Corum – certain beings have been released who would not otherwise have the power they now possess. And possessing great power, they crave for more – for all the power that there is in our universe. These beings are amoral in a way in which the Lords of Law and Chaos are not. They do not fight for influence upon the Earth, as those gods do. Their only wish is to convert the essential energy of our universe to their own uses. I believe they foster some ambition in their particular universe which would be furthered if they could achieve their wish. At present, in spite of conditions highly favourable to them, they have not attained their full strength, but the time is not far off before they do attain it. Agak and Gagak is how they are called in human tongue and they are outside the power of any of our gods, so a more powerful group has been summoned – yourselves.'

Hawkmoon made to ask how they could be more powerful than gods, but he controlled the impulse.

'The Champion Eternal,' the Captain continued, 'in four of his incarnations (and four is the maximum number we can risk without precipitating further unwelcome disruptions amongst the planes of Earth) – Erekosë, Elric, Corum and Hawkmoon. Each of you will command four others, whose fates are linked with your own and who are great fighters in their own right, though they do not share your destinies in every sense. You may each pick the four with whom you wish to fight. I think you will find it easy enough to decide. We make landfall quite shortly now.'

Hawkmoon wondered if he disliked the Captain. He felt that he challenged him when he said: 'You will lead us?'

The Captain seemed genuinely regretful. 'I cannot. I can only take you to the island and wait for those who survive – if any survive.'

Elric frowned, voicing Hawkmoon's own reservations. 'This fight is not mine, I think.'

But the Captain's answer was given with conviction, with authority. 'It is yours – and it is mine. I would land with you if that were permitted me, but it is not.'

'Why so?' This was Corum speaking.

'You will learn that one day.' A cloud seemed to pass over the Captain's blind features. 'I have not the courage to tell you. I bear you nothing but good will, however. Be assured of that.'

Hawkmoon found himself thinking cynically, once again, about the value of assurances.

'Well,' said Erekosë, 'since it is my destiny to fight, and since I, like Hawkmoon, continue to seek Tanelorn, and since I gather there is some chance of my fulfilling my ambition if I am successful, I for one agree to go against these two, Agak and Gagak.'

Hawkmoon shrugged and nodded. 'I go with Erekosë – for similar reasons.'

Corum sighed. 'And I.'

Elric looked about him at the other three. 'Not long

since, I counted myself without comrades. Now I have many. For that reason alone I will fight with them.'

Erekosë was pleased by this. 'It is perhaps the best of reasons.'

The Captain spoke again, his blind eyes seeming to stare beyond them. 'There is no reward for this work, save my assurance that your success will save the world much misery. And for you, Elric, there is less reward than the rest may hope for.'

Elric seemed to disagree, but Hawkmoon could not read the albino's face when he said, 'Perhaps not.'

'As you say.' The Captain's tone had changed. He was more relaxed. 'More wine, my friends?'

They drank the wine he offered them and waited while he continued. His face was raised now. He addressed the sky, his voice distant.

'Upon this island is a ruin – perhaps it was once a city called Tanelorn – and at the centre of the ruin stands one whole building. It is this building which Agak and his sister use. It is that which you must attack. You will recognize it, I hope, at once.'

'And we must slay this pair?' Erekosë spoke as if the work were nothing.

'If you can. They have servants who help them. These must be slain, also. Then the building must be fired. This is important.' The Captain paused. 'Fired. It must be destroyed in no other way.'

Hawkmoon noticed that Elric was smiling. 'There are few other ways of destroying buildings, Sir Captain.'

It seemed a pointless observation to Hawkmoon and he thought that the Captain responded with great politeness, bowing slightly and saying, 'Aye, it's so. Nonetheless, it is worth remembering what I have said.'

'Do you know what these two look like, these Agak and Gagak?' said Corum.

The Captain shook his head. 'No. It is possible that they

resemble creatures of our own worlds. It is possible that they do not. Few have seen them. It is only recently that they have been able to materialize at all.'

'And how may they best be overwhelmed?' Hawkmoon spoke almost banteringly.

'By courage and ingenuity,' the Captain said.

'You are not very explicit, sir,' said Elric in a tone which echoed Hawkmoon's.

'I am as explicit as I can be. Now, my friends, I suggest you rest and prepare your arms.'

They issued into the writhing mist. It clung to the ship like a desperate beast. It stirred. It threatened them.

Erekosë's mood had changed. 'We have little free will,' he said morosely, 'for all we deceive ourselves otherwise. If we perish or live through this venture, it will not count for much in the overall scheme of things.'

'I think you are of a gloomy turn of mind, friend,' Hawkmoon told him sardonically. He would have continued, but Corum interrupted.

'A realistic turn of mind.'

They reached the cabin shared by Erekosë and Elric. Corum and Hawkmoon left them there and tramped up the deck, through the white, clinging stuff, to their own cabin, there to pick the four who would follow them.

'We are the Four Who Are One,' said Corum. 'We have great power. I know that we have great power.'

But Hawkmoon was wearying of talk he found altogether too mystical for his own, normally practical, turn of mind.

He hefted the sword he was honing. 'This is the most trustworthy power,' he said. 'Sharp steel.'

Many of the other warriors murmured their agreement.

'We shall see,' said Corum.

But as he polished the blade, Hawkmoon could not help but be reminded of the outline of that other sword he had observed beneath Elric's cloak. He knew that he would recognize it when he saw it. He did not know, however, why he feared it so much, and this lack of knowledge also disturbed him. He found himself thinking of Yisselda, of Yarmila and Manfred, of Count Brass and the Heroes of the Kamarg. This adventure had begun partly because he had hoped to find all his old comrades and loved ones again. Now he was threatened with never seeing any of them again. And yet it was worth fighting in the Captain's cause if Tanelorn, and consequently his children, could be found. And where was Yisselda? Would he find her, too, in Tanelorn?

Soon they were ready. Hawkmoon had with him John ap-Rhyss, Emshon of Ariso, Keeth Woecarrier and Turning Nikhe, while Baron Gotterin, Thereod of the Caves, Chaz of Elaquol and Reingir the Rock, awakened at last from his drunken snoozings and stumbling blearily in the wake of the rest, made up Corum's party. Privately, Hawkmoon felt he had the pick of the men.

Into the mist they marched, and to the side of the ship. The anchor was already rattling, the ship already settling. They could see rocky land – an isle which looked distinctly inhospitable. Could it possibly shelter Tanelorn the fabulous city of peace?

John ap-Rhyss sniffed suspiciously, wiping the mist from his moustache, his other hand playing with the hilt of his sword. 'I have seen no place less welcoming,' he said.

The Captain had left his cabin. His steersman stood next to him. Both held armfuls of brands.

With a shock, Hawkmoon saw that the steersman's face was the twin of the Captain's – but the eyes were not blind. They were sharp, they were full of knowledge. Hawkmoon could hardly bear to look at the face as he accepted his brand and tucked it into his belt.

'Only fire will destroy this enemy forever.' The Captain now handed Hawkmoon a tinder box with which to light the brand when the time came. 'I wish you success, warriors.'

Now each man had a brand and a tinder box. Erekosë was first over the side, swinging down the rope ladder, unclipping his sword so that it would not touch the water, and plunging into the milky sea up to his waist. The others followed him, wading through the shallows until they stood upon the shore, looking back at the ship.

Hawkmoon noticed that the mist did not extend as far as the land, which had now taken on some colour. Normally, he would have thought how dull the surroundings were, but in contrast to the ship they were bright – red rocks festooned with lichen of several shades of yellow. And above his head was a great disc, bloody and still, which was the sun. It cast a great many shadows, thought Hawkmoon.

It was only slowly that he began to notice just how many shadows were cast – shadows which could not possibly belong to the rocks alone – shadows of all sizes, of all shapes.

Some, he saw, were the shadows of men.

4

A CITY HAUNTED BY ITSELF

The sky was like a wound gone bad, full of dreadful, unhealthy blues, browns, dark reds and yellows, and there were shadows in it which, unlike those on the land, sometimes moved.

One called Hown Serpent-tamer, a member of Elric's party, whose armour was sea-green and scintillating, said: 'I have rarely been ashore, it's true, but I think the quality of this land is stranger than any other I've known. It shimmers. It distorts.'

'Aye,' said Hawkmoon. He had noticed the same sweep of flickering light which passed from time to time over the island and distorted the outlines of the surrounding ground.

A barbaric warrior, with braids and glaring eyes, called Ashnar the Lynx, was plainly much discomforted by all of this. 'And from whence come all these shadows?' he growled. 'Why cannot we see that which casts them?'

They continued to march inland, though all were reluctant to leave the shore and the ship behind. Corum seemed the least disturbed. He spoke in a tone of philosophical curiosity.

'It could be that these are shadows cast by objects existing in other dimensions of the Earth,' said the Prince in the Scarlet Robe. 'If all dimensions meet here, as has been suggested, that could be a likely explanation. This is not the strangest example I have witnessed of such a conjunction.'

A black man, whose face bore a peculiar V-shaped scar, and who was called Otto Blendker, fingered the sword belt which crossed his chest and grunted. 'Likely? Pray let none give me an *unlikely* explanation, if you please!'

Thereod of the Caves said: 'I have witnessed a similar peculiarity in the deepest caves of my own land, but nothing so vast. There, I was told, dimensions met. So Corum is doubtless right.' He shifted the long, slender sword on his back. He spoke no more to the party in general, but fell to conversing with the dwarfish Emshon of Ariso who was, as usual, grumbling about something.

Hawkmoon was still considering if they had been duped by the Captain. They still had no proof that the blind man truly meant them well. For all Hawkmoon knew the Captain himself had designs upon the worlds and was using them against their fellows. But he voiced nothing of this to the others, all of whom seemed prepared to do the Captain's bidding without question.

Once more Hawkmoon found himself eyeing the shape of the sword beneath Elric's cloak and wondering why it perturbed him so much. He became lost in his own thoughts, looking as little as possible at the disturbing landscape around him, reviewing the events which had led to his finding himself in this company. He was aroused from his reverie by Corum's voice saying:

'Perhaps this is Tanelorn – or, rather, all the versions of Tanelorn there have ever been. For Tanelorn exists in many forms, each form depending upon the wishes of those who most desire to find her.'

Hawkmoon looked and he saw the city. It was a crazy assortment of ruins, displaying every possible idiosyncratic style of architecture, as if some god had collected examples of buildings from every world of the multiverse and placed them here, willy-nilly. All were in ruins. They stretched away to the horizon – tottering towers, shattered minarets, crumbling castles – and all cast shadows. Moreover, in this city, too, there were many shadows which had no apparent origin. Shadows of buildings not visible to their eyes.

Hawkmoon was shocked. 'This is not the Tanelorn I

expected to find,' he said.

'Nor I.' Erekosë spoke in a tone which echoed Hawkmoon's.

'Perhaps it is not Tanelorn.' Elric stopped short, his crimson eyes scanning the ruins. 'Perhaps it is not.'

'Or perhaps this is a graveyard.' Corum frowned. 'A graveyard containing all the forgotten versions of that strange city?'

Hawkmoon refused to pause. He kept walking until he had reached the ruins, and the others began to follow him, until they were all clambering through the broken stones, inspecting here a piece of engraving, there a fallen statue. Behind him, Hawkmoon heard Erekosë speaking in a low voice to Elric.

'Have you noticed,' said Erekosë, 'that the shadows now represent something.'

Hawkmoon heard Elric reply. 'You can tell from the ruins what some of the buildings looked like when they were whole. The shadows are the shadows of those buildings – the original buildings before they became ruined.'

Hawkmoon looked for himself and saw that Elric was right. It was a city haunted by itself.

'Just so,' said Erekosë.

Hawkmoon turned. 'We were promised Tanelorn. We were promised a corpse!'

'Possibly,' said Corum, thoughtfully. 'But do not come to too hasty a conclusion, Hawkmoon.'

'I would judge the centre to be over there, ahead of us,' said John ap-Rhyss. 'Would that be the best place to look for those we fight?'

The others agreed and they altered the direction of their march a little, making for a cleared space amongst the ruins where a building could be seen, its outline sharp and clean where the outlines of the others were indistinct. Its colours, too, were brighter, with planes of curved metal going at all angles, connected by tubes which might have been of crystal and which glowed and throbbed.

'It resembles a machine more than a building,' Hawkmoon found his curiosity aroused.

'And a musical instrument more than a machine.' Corum's single eye viewed the building with a certain awe.

The four heroes stopped and their men stopped with them.

'This must be the dwelling of the sorcerers,' said Emshon of Ariso. 'They do themselves well, eh? And look – it is really two identical buildings, connected by those tubes.'

'A home for the brother and a home for the sister,' said Reingir the Rock. He belched and looked apologetic.

'Two buildings,' Erekosë remarked. 'We were not prepared for this. Shall we split up and attack both?'

Elric shook his head. 'I think we should go together into one, else our strength will be weakened.'

'I agree,' said Hawkmoon, wishing he knew why he was so reluctant, nonetheles, to follow Elric into the building.

'Well, let us set to it,' Baron Gotterin said. 'Let us enter Hell, if this is not Hell already.'

Corum gave the Baron an amused glance. 'You are certainly determined to prove your theory!'

Again Hawkmoon took the initiative, heading over the level ground towards what he guessed to be the doorway of the nearest building – a dark, asymmetrical gash. As the twenty warriors approached, experienced eyes wary for attack by any possible defenders, the building seemed to take on a brighter glow, seemed to pulse with a steady beat, seemed to emit peculiar, almost inaudible, whispering noises. Used to the sorcerous technology of the Dark Empire, Hawkmoon still found himself fearing the place, and suddenly he was holding back, letting Elric lead the way in, his four chosen comrades with him. Hawkmoon and his men went next through the black portal and they were in a passage which curved sharply almost as soon as they had entered; a humid passage which brought sweat to their faces. Again they paused, glancing at one another. Then they began to move again, ready to meet whatever defenders there were.

They had gone some distance along the passage before its walls and floor began to shake so heavily that Hown Serpent-tamer was flung downwards, to lie sprawled and swearing while the others barely managed to keep their balance, and at the same time there came a booming, faraway voice from ahead – a voice full of querulous outrage.

'Who? Who? Who?'

Hawkmoon, gripped by inapposite humour, thought it the voice of a mad and gigantic owl.

'Who? Who? Who invades me?'

With the help of the others, Hown had regained his footing. They pushed on as the passage's motion became somewhat less violent, while the voice continued to mutter, distracted, as if to itself.

'What attacks? What?'

None had any explanation for the voice. All were bewildered by it. They said nothing, letting Elric lead them into a fairly large hall.

Within the hall the air was even warmer and hard to breathe. Viscous fluid dripped from the ceiling and oozed down the walls. Hawkmoon found himself disgusted and quelled a strong desire to turn back. Then Ashnar the Lynx yelped and pointed at the beasts which squeezed themselves through the walls and came slithering at them, mouths gaping. They were snake-like things and the sight of them brought bile to Hawkmoon's throat.

'Attack!' The voice cried again. 'Destroy this! Destroy it!' There was a terrible, mindless quality to the command.

Instinctively the warriors formed themselves into four groups, standing back to back to meet the attack.

Instead of real teeth, the beasts had sharp bone ridges in their mouths, like twin knives, making a horrid clashing sound as they drew their shapeless, disgusting bodies through the slime of the floor.

Elric was the first to draw his sword and Hawkmoon was distracted for a second as he saw the huge black blade rise over the albino's head. He could have sworn that he heard the blade moan, that it glowed with a life which was its own. But then he was cutting at the beasts which slithered all around him, striking into flesh which parted with nauseating ease and which gave off a stink threatening to overwhelm them all. The air grew thicker and the fluid on the floor was deeper and Elric was shouting to them. 'Move on through them!' he cried. 'Hacking a path through as you go. Head for yonder opening.'

Hawkmoon saw the doorway and he knew that Elric's plan was the best they could hope for. He began to press forward, his men moving with him, destroying a multitude of the horrid beasts as they went. As a result the stench increased and Hawkmoon was gagging now.

'The creatures are not hard to fight!' Hown Serpent-tamer was panting. 'But each one we kill robs us a little of our own chances of life.'

'Cunningly planned by our enemies, no doubt,' answered Elric.

Elric was the first to reach the passage, waving them to join him.

Thrusting, swinging, slicing, they gained the door and the beasts were reluctant to follow. Here the air was a little more breathable. Hawkmoon leaned against the wall of the passage, listening to the others debate, but unable to join the conversation.

'*Attack! Attack!*' ordered the faraway voice. But no further attack came.

'I like not this castle at all.' Brut of Lashmar fingered a tear in his cloak. 'High sorcery commands it.'

'It is only what we knew,' said Ashnar the Lynx, his barbarian's eyes darting this way and that.

Otto Blendker, another of Elric's men, wiped sweat from his black brow. 'They are cowards, these sorcerers. They do not show themselves.' He was almost shouting. 'Is their aspect so loathsome that they are afraid lest we look upon them?' Hawkmoon realized that Blendker was speaking for the benefit of the two sorcerers, Agak and Gagak, hoping to shame them into appearing. But there was no response. Soon they were pushing on through the fleshy passages, which changed dimensions frequently and were sometimes all but impassable. The light, too, was inconstant, and often they moved in complete darkness, linking hands so as not to become separated.

'The floor rises all the time,' murmured Hawkmoon to John ap-Rhyss, who was nearest to him. 'We must be fairly close to the top of the building.'

ap-Rhyss made no reply. His teeth were clenched as if he tried not to betray his fear.

'The Captain said that the sorcerers could probably change shape,' Emshon of Ariso said. 'They must change frequently, for these passages are not designed for creatures of any one particular size.'

Elric, at the head of the twenty, said: 'I become impatient to confront these shape changers.'

Ashnar the Lynx, next to him, growled: 'They said there'd be treasure here. I thought to stake my life against a fair reward, but there's nought here of value.' He touched the wall. 'Not even stone or brick. What are these walls made of, Elric?'

Hawkmoon had wondered the same thing and he hoped that the albino would offer an explanation, but Elric was shaking his head. 'That has puzzled me, also, Ashnar.'

Hawkmoon heard Elric draw in his breath, saw him raise his strange, heavy sword – and there were new attackers coming at them. These were beasts with red,

78

snarling mouths and their bristling fur was orange. Yellow fangs dripped saliva. Elric was the first to be threatened, driving his sword deep into the first beast's belly even as its claws fell on him. It was like a huge baboon and the thrust had not killed it.

Then Hawkmoon was engaged with another of the apes, slashing at it while it feinted, side-stepping his blows, and Hawkmoon was aware that he had little chance, individually, against it. He saw Keeth Woecarrier, careless of his safety, come blundering to his aid, big sword swinging, a look of resignation upon his melancholy face. The ape turned its attention to the Woecarrier, throwing the whole weight of its body at him. Keeth's blade ran it through the chest, but its fangs were on the large man's throat and blood was bursting from the jugular almost in an instant.

Hawkmoon thrust under the ape's ribs, knowing that it was too late to save Keeth Woecarrier whose body was already sinking to the damp floor. Corum appeared, stabbing the creature from the other side. It snarled, turning on them, claws reaching for them. Its eyes glazed. It stumbled. It fell backwards on to the Woecarrier's corpse.

Hawkmoon did not wait to be attacked, but sprang over the corpses to where Baron Gotterin was locked in the grip of another orange ape. Teeth snapped, tearing the fat face free of the skull. Gotterin yelled once, almost in triumph, almost as if he felt his theory vindicated. Then he died. Ashnar the Lynx used his sword like an axe, lopping off the head of Gotterin's assassin. He stood upon the body of another slain ape. Miraculously, he had taken two of the beasts singlehanded. He was roaring out some toneless battle song. He was full of joy now.

Hawkmoon grinned at the barbarian and rushed to Corum's assistance, making a deep cut through the neck and back of the baboon. Blood shot into his eyes and blinded him for a moment so that he thought he was doomed. But the beast was finished. It twitched for only a few seconds longer. Corum pushed it from him with the pommel of his sword.

Hawkmoon saw that Chaz of Elaquol was also dead, but that Turning Nikhe still lived, nursing a deep gash in his face, grinning the while. Reingir the Rock lay upon his back, his throat torn out, while John ap-Rhyss, Emshon of Ariso and Thereod of the Caves had managed to survive the fight with only minor wounds. Erekosë's men had fared less well. One had his arm hanging by strips of flesh alone, another had lost an eye and another had had his hand bitten clean off. The others were tending them as best they could. Brut of Lashmar, Hown Serpent-tamer, Ashnar the Lynx and Otto Blendker were also reasonably unhurt.

Ashnar looked triumphantly upon the bodies of the two apes. 'I begin to suspect this venture of being uneconomical,' he said. He was panting as a hound might pant after a successful kill. 'The less time we take over it, the better. What think you, Elric?'

'I would agree.' Elric shook blood from his fearsome sword. 'Come.'

Without waiting for the others, he began to lead the way towards a chamber ahead. The chamber glowed with a peculiar pink light. Hawkmoon and the others followed him into it.

Now Elric was looking down in horror. He bent and grasped something. And Hawkmoon felt his own legs seized. They were snakes, covering the floor of the chamber – long, thin reptiles, flesh-coloured and eyeless – tightening their coils about his ankles. Wildly, Hawkmoon hacked downwards, severing two or three of the heads, but the coils did not relax. Around him, his surviving comrades were shouting with fear, trying to free themselves.

And then the one called Hown Serpent-tamer, the

warrior in the sea-green armour, began to sing.

He sang in a voice which was like the sound of a waterfall in a mountain stream. He sang casually, for all the urgency in the set of his face, and slowly the snakes began to release their hold upon the men, slowly they fell back to the floor, appearing to sleep.

'Now I understand how you came by your surname,' said Elric in relief.

'I was not sure the song would work on these,' said the Serpent-tamer, 'for they are unlike any serpents I have ever seen in the seas of my own world.'

They left the snakes behind, climbing higher, finding it difficult to keep a purchase on the yielding, slimy floor. The heat was increasing all the time and Hawkmoon felt that he might faint if he did not soon breathe fresher air. He became reconciled to going down on his stomach in order to squeeze through tiny, rubbery gaps in the passage; to spreading his arms at times in order to maintain his balance as tall caverns shook and rained sticky liquid on his head; to slapping at small creatures, rather like insects, which from time to time attacked; to hearing the sourceless voice crying:

'Where? Where? Oh, the pain!'

The little beasts flew around them in clouds, nipping at their faces and hands, hardly visible yet always present.

'Where?'

Virtually blinded, Hawkmoon forced his body on, restraining the urge to vomit, desperate for sweet air, seeing warriors fall and being hardly able to help them up again. Upward, higher and higher, rose the passage, twisting in every direction, and Hown Serpent-tamer continued to sing, for there were still many snakes on the floor.

Ashnar the Lynx had lost his short-lived ebullience. 'We can survive this only a little longer. We shall be in no condition to meet the sorcerer if we ever find him or his sister.'

'My thoughts, too,' said Elric. 'Yet what else may we do, Ashnar?'

'Nothing,' Hawkmoon heard Ashnar murmur. 'Nothing.'

And the same word was repeated, sometimes louder, sometimes softer:

'*Where?*' it said.

'*Where?*' it demanded.

'*Where? Where? Where?*'

And soon the voice had grown to a shout. It rang in Hawkmoon's ears. It grated on his nerves.

'Here,' he muttered. 'Here we are, sorcerer.'

Then they had come to the end of the passage at last and saw an archway of regular proportions, and beyond the archway a well-lit chamber.

'Agak's room, without doubt,' said Ashnar the Lynx.

They stepped into an octagonal chamber.

5

AGAK AND GAGAK

There were eight milky colours to each of the eight inwardly sloping sides of the chamber; each colour changing in unison with the others. From time to time a side would become almost transparent and it was possible to see through it to the ruins of the city below, the other building, still connected by a network of tubes and threads.

There were noises within the chamber – a sighing, a whispering, a bubbling. They came from a great pool set into the centre of the floor.

Reluctantly, they filed into the chamber. Reluctantly they looked into the pool and saw that the substance there might be the stuff of life itself, for it moved constantly, it formed shapes – faces, bodies, limbs of all manner of men and beasts; structures which rivalled those of the city outside for architectural variety; whole landscapes in miniature; unfamiliar firmaments, suns and planets; creatures of unlikely beauty and of convincing ugliness; scenes of battles, of families at peace in their households, of harvests, ceremonies, pomp; ships both outlandish and familiar, some of which flew through the skies, or through the darks of space, or below the waves, in nameless materials, unusual timbers, peculiar metals.

In fascination, Hawkmoon stared and stared, until a voice roared from the pool, revealing its source at last.

'WHAT? WHAT? WHO INVADES?'

Hawkmoon saw Elric's face in the pool. He saw Corum's face there and he saw Erekosë's. When he recognized his own, he turned away.

'WHO INVADES? AH! I AM TOO WEAK!'

Elric was the first to reply:

'We are of those you would destroy. We are those on whom you would feed.'

'AH! AGAK! AGAK! I AM SICK! WHERE ARE YOU?'

Hawkmoon exchanged puzzled glances with Corum and with Erekosë. None could explain the sorcerer's response.

Shapes rose from the liquid and fell apart, fell back into the pool.

Hawkmoon saw Yisselda there, and other women who reminded him of Yisselda, though they did not resemble her. He cried out, starting forward. Erekosë restrained him. The figures of the women disintegrated and were replaced by the twisting towers of an alien city.

'I WEAKEN . . . MY ENERGY NEEDS TO BE REPLENISHED . . . WE MUST BEGIN NOW, AGAK . . . IT TOOK US SO LONG TO REACH THIS PLACE. I THOUGHT I COULD REST. BUT THERE IS DISEASE HERE. IT FILLS MY BODY. AGAK. AWAKEN AGAK. AWAKEN!'

Hawkmoon controlled the shudders which began to rack his body.

Elric was staring intently into the pool, an expression of dawning realization on his pale face.

'Some servant of Agak's, charged with the defence of the chamber?' This was Hown Serpent-tamer's suggestion.

'Will Agak wake?' Brut glanced around the eight-sided chamber. 'Will he come?'

'Agak!' Ashnar the Lynx raised his braided head in a challenge. 'Coward!'

'Agak!' cried John ap-Rhyss, drawing his sword.

'Agak!' shouted Emshon of Ariso.

The others all took up the shout; all save the four heroes.

Hawkmoon was beginning to guess what the words had meant. And something was growing inside his mind –

another understanding, an understanding of how the sorcerers must be slain. His lips formed the word 'No', but could not voice it. He looked again into the faces of the three other aspects of the Champion Eternal. He saw that the others were also afraid.

'We are the Four Who Are One.' Erekosë's voice was shaking.

'No . . .' Elric spoke now. He was making some sort of attempt to sheath his black sword, but the sword seemed to be refusing to enter the scabbard. There was panic and horror in the albino's crimson eyes.

Hawkmoon took a small step backward, hating the images which now filled his head, hating the impulse which had seized his will.

'AGAK! QUICKLY!'

The pool boiled.

Hawkmoon heard Erekosë saying:

'If we do not do this thing, they will eat all our worlds. Nothing will remain.'

Hawkmoon did not care.

Elric, closest to the pool, was clutching his bone-white head and swaying, threatening to fall. Hawkmoon made a movement towards him, hearing the albino groan, hearing Corum's urgent, echoing voice behind him, feeling desperate, wholehearted comradeship with his three counterparts.

'We must do it then,' said Corum.

Elric was panting. 'I will not,' he said. 'I am myself.'

'And I!' Hawkmoon stretched out a hand, but Elric did not see it.

'It is the only way for us,' said Corum, 'for the single thing that we are. Do you not see that? We are the only creatures of our worlds who possess the means of slaying the sorcerers – in the only manner in which they can be slain!'

Hawkmoon's eyes met Elric's; they met those of Corum;

they met Erekosë's. The Hawkmoon knew and the
individual that was Hawkmoon recoiled from the knowledge.

'We are the Four Who Are One,' Erekosë's tones were
firm. 'Our united strength is greater than the sum. We
must come together, brothers. We must conquer here
before we can hope to conquer Agak.'

'No . . .' said Elric, voicing Hawkmoon's emotion.

But something greater than Hawkmoon was at work
within him. He moved to one corner of the pool and stood
there, seeing that the others had taken up positions at each
of the other corners.

'AGAK!' said the voice. 'AGAK!' And the pool's
activity became more violent.

Hawkmoon could not speak. He saw that the faces of his
three counterparts were as frozen as his own. He was only
dimly aware of the warriors who had followed them here.
They were moving away from the pool, guarding the
entrance, looking about them for signs of attack, protect-
ing the Four, but their eyes held terror.

Hawkmoon saw the great black sword move upwards,
but he could feel no more fear of it as his own sword rose
to meet it. Then all four swords were touching, their tips
meeting over the exact centre of the pool.

At the moment when the tips met, Hawkmoon gasped,
feeling a power fill his soul. He heard Elric's shout and
knew that the albino was experiencing the same sensation.
Hawkmoon hated the power. It enslaved him. He wished
to escape from it, even now.

'*I understand.*' It was Corum's voice, but the lips were
Hawkmoon's. '*It is the only way.*'

'*Oh no, no!*' And Hawkmoon's voice sprang from Elric's
throat.

Hawkmoon felt his name go away.

'AGAK! AGAK!' The substance of the pool writhed,
boiled and leaped. 'QUICKLY! WAKE!'

Hawkmoon knew that his identity was fading. He was Elric. He was Erekosë. He was Corum. And he was Hawkmoon, too. A little of him was still Hawkmoon. And he was a thousand others – Urlik, Jherek, Asquiol . . . He was a part of a gigantic, a noble beast . . .

His body had changed. He hovered over the pool. The vestige of Hawkmoon could see it for a second before that vestige joined the central being.

On each side of its head was a face and each face belonged to one of the companions. Serene and terrible, the eyes did not blink. It had eight arms and the arms were still; it squatted over the pool on eight legs, and its armour and accoutrements were of all colours blending and at the same time separate.

The being clutched a single great sword in all eight hands and both he and the sword glowed with a ghastly golden light.

'Ah,' he thought, '*now I am whole.*'

The Four Who Were One reversed its monstrous sword so that the point was directed downward at the frenetically boiling stuff in the pool below. The stuff feared the sword. It mewled.

'*Agak, Agak . . .*'

The being of whom Hawkmoon was a part gathered its great strength and began to plunge the sword down.

Shapeless waves appeared on the surface of the pool. Its whole colour changed from sickly yellow to an unhealthy green. '*Agak, I die . . .*'

Inexorably the sword moved down. It touched the surface.

The pool swept back and forth; it tried to ooze over the sides and on to the floor. The sword bit deeper and the Four Who Were One felt new strength flow up the blade. There came a moan; slowly the pool quietened. It became silent. It became still. It became grey.

Then the Four Who Were One descended into the pool

to be absorbed.

Hawkmoon rode for Londra and with him were Huillam D'Averc, Yisselda of Brass, Oladahn of the Bulgar Mountains, Bowgentle the philosopher, and Count Brass. Each of these wore a mirror helm which reflected the rays of the sun.

Hawkmoon held the Horn of Fate in his hands. He put it to his lips. He blew the blast to herald in the night of the new earth. The night that would precede the new dawn. And though the horn's note was triumphant, Hawkmoon was not. He stood full of infinite loneliness and infinite sorrow, his head tilted back as the sound rang on.

Hawkmoon relived the torment he had suffered in the forest, when Glandyth had struck off his hand. He screamed as the pain came to his wrist once more and then there was fire in his face and he knew that Kwll had plucked his brother's jewelled eye from his skull, now that his powers were restored. Red darkness swam in his brain. Red fire drained his energy. Red pain consumed his flesh.

And Hawkmoon spoke in tones of the most terrible torment. 'Which of the names will I have next time you call?'

'Now Earth is peaceful. The silent air carries only the sounds of quiet laughter, the murmur of conversation, the small noises of small animals. We and Earth are at peace.'

'But how long can it last?'

'Oh, how long can it last?'

The beast that was the Champion Eternal could see clearly now.

It tested its body. It controlled every limb, every function. It had triumphed; it had revitalized the pool.

Through its single octagonal eye it looked in all directions at the same time over the wide ruins of the city; then it focused all its attention upon its twin.

Agak had awakened too late, but he was awakening at

last, roused by the dying cries of his sister Gagak whose body the mortals had first invaded and whose intelligence they had overwhelmed, whose eye they now used and whose powers they would soon attempt to utilize.

Agak did not need to turn his head to look upon the being he still saw as his sister. Like hers, his intelligence was contained within the huge octagonal eye.

'Did you call me, sister?'

'I spoke your name, that is all, brother.' There were enough vestiges of Gagak's lifeforce in the Four Who Were One for it to imitate her manner of speaking.

'You cried out?'

'A dream.' The Four paused and then it spoke again: *'A disease. I dreamed that there was something upon this island which made me unwell.'*

'Is that possible? We do not know sufficient about these dimensions or the creatures inhabiting them. Yet none is as powerful as Agak and Gagak. Fear not, sister. We must begin our work soon.'

'It is nothing. Now I am awake.'

Agak was puzzled. *'You speak oddly.'*

'The dream . . .' answered the creature which had entered Gagak's body and destroyed her.

'We must begin,' said Agak. *'The dimensions turn and the time has come. Ah, I feel it. It waits for us to take it. So much rich energy. How we shall conquer when we go home!'*

'I feel it,' replied the Four, and it did.

It felt its whole universe, dimension upon dimension, swirling all about it. Stars and planets and moons through plane upon plane, all full of the energy upon which Agak and Gagak had desired to feed. And there was enough of Gagak still within the Four to make the Four experience a deep, anticipatory hunger which, now that the dimensions attained the right conjunction, would soon be satisfied.

The Four was tempted to join with Agak and feast, though it knew if it did so it would rob its own universe of

89

every shred of energy. Stars would fade, worlds would die. Even the Lords of Law and Chaos would perish, for they were part of the same universe. Yet to possess such power it might be worth committing such a tremendous crime . . .

It controlled this desire and gathered itself for its attack before Agak became too wary.

'Shall we feast, sister?'

The Four realized that the ship had brought it to the island at exactly the proper moment. Indeed, they had almost come too late.

'Sister?' Agak was again puzzled. *'What . . .?'*

The Four knew it must disconnect from Agak. The tubes and wires fell away from his body and were withdrawn into Gagak's.

'What's this?' Agak's strange body trembled for a moment. *'Sister?'*

The Four prepared itself. For all that it had absorbed Gagak's memories and instincts, it was still not confident that it would be able to attack Agak in her chosen form. And since the sorceress had possessed the power to change her form, the Four began to change, groaning greatly, experiencing dreadful pain, drawing all the materials of its stolen being together so that what had appeared to be a building now became pulpy, unformed flesh. And Agak, stunned, looked on.

'Sister? Your Sanity . . .'

The building, the creature that was Gagak, threshed, melted and erupted.

It screamed in agony.

It attained its form.

It laughed.

6

THE BATTLE FOR EVERYTHING

Four faces laughed upon a gigantic head. Eight arms waved in triumph, eight legs began to move. And over that head it waved a single, massive sword.

And it was running.

It ran upon Agak while the alien sorcerer was still in his static form. Its sword was whirling and shards of ghastly golden light fell away from it as it moved, lashing the shadowed landscape. The Four was as large as Agak. And at this moment it was as strong.

But Agak, realizing his danger, began to suck. No longer would this be a pleasurable ritual shared with his sister. He must suck at the energy of this universe if he was to find the strength to defend himself, to gain what he needed to destroy his attacker, the slayer of his sister.

Worlds died as Agak sucked.

But not enough.

Agak tried cunning:

'This is the centre of your universe. All its dimensions intersect here. Come, you can share the power. My sister is dead. I accept her death. You shall be my partner now. With this power we shall conquer a universe far richer than this!'

'No!' said the Four, still advancing.

'Very well, but be assured of your defeat.'

The Four swung its sword. The sword fell upon the faceted eye within which Agak's intelligence pool bubbled, just as his sister's had once bubbled. But Agak was stronger already and healed himself at once.

Agak's tendrils emerged and lashed at the Four and the Four cut at the tendrils as they sought its body. And Agak sucked more energy to himself. His body, which the

91

mortals had mistaken for a building, began to glow burning scarlet and to radiate an impossible heat.

The sword roared and flared so that black light mingled with the gold and flowed against the scarlet.

And all the while the Four could sense its own universe shrinking and dying.

'Give back, Agak, what you have stolen!' said the Four.

Planes and angles and curves, wires and tubes, flickered with deep red heat and Agak sighed. The universe whimpered.

'*I am stronger than you*,' said Agak. '*Now!*'

The Four knew that Agak's attention was diverted for just that short while as he fed. And the Four knew that it, too, must draw energy from its own universe if Agak were to be defeated. So the sword was raised.

The sword was flung back, its blade slicing through tens of thousands of dimensions and drawing their power to it. Then it began to swing back.

It swung and black light bellowed from its blade.

It swung and Agak became aware of it. His body began to alter.

Down towards the sorcerer's great eye, down towards Agak's intelligence pool swept the black blade.

Agak's many tendrils rose to defend the sorcerer against the sword, but the sword cut through them as if they were not there and it struck the eight-sided chamber which was Agak's eye and it plunged on down into Agak's intelligence pool, deep into the stuff of the sorcerer's sensibility, drawing up Agak's energy into itself and thence into its master, the Four Who Were One.

And something screamed through the universe.

And something sent a tremor through the universe.

And the universe was dead, even as Agak began to die.

The Four did not dare wait to see if Agak were completely vanquished.

It swept the sword out, back through the dimensions, and everywhere the blade touched the energy was restored.

The sword rang round and round.

Round and round. Dispersing the energy.

And the sword sang its triumph and its glee.

And little shreds of black and golden light whispered away and were re-absorbed.

Hawkmoon knew the nature of the Champion. He knew the nature of the Black Sword. He knew the nature of Tanelorn. For at this moment that part of him which was Hawkmoon had experience of the whole multiverse. It inhabited him. He contained it. There were no mysteries at that moment.

And he recalled that one of his aspects had read something in the Chronicle of the Black Sword, that record of the Champion's exploits: 'For the Mind of Man alone is free to explore the lofty vastness of the cosmic infinite, to transcend ordinary consciousness, or roam the subterranean corridors of the human brain with its boundless dimensions. And universe and individual are linked, the one mirrored in the other, and each contains the other . . .'

'Ha!' cried that individual which was Hawkmoon. And he triumphed; he celebrated. This was the end to the Champion's doom!

For a moment the universe had been dead. Now it lived and Agak's energy had been added to it.

Agak lived, too, but he was frozen. He had attempted to change his shape. Now he still half resembled the building Hawkmoon had seen when he first came to the island, but part of him resembled the Four Who Were One. Here was part of Corum's face, here a leg, there a fragment of sword blade – as if Agak had believed, at the end, that the Four could only be defeated if its own form were assumed, just as the Four had assumed Gagak's form.

'*We had waited so long . . .*' Agak sighed and then he was dead.

And the Four sheathed its sword.

Hawkmoon thought . . .

Then came a howling through the ruins of the many cities and a strong wind blustered against the body of the Four so that it was forced to kneel on its eight legs and bow its four-faced head before the gale.

Hawkmoon felt . . .

Then, gradually, it assumed again the shape of Gagak, the sorceress, and then it lay within Gagak's stagnating intelligence pool . . .

Hawkmoon knew . . .

. . . and then it rose over it, hovered for a moment, withdrew its sword from the pool.

Hawkmoon was Hawkmoon. Hawkmoon was the Champion Eternal on his last great quest . . .

Then four beings fled apart and Elric and Hawkmoon and Erekosë and Corum stood with sword blades touching over the centre of the dead brain.

Hawkmoon sighed. He was full of wonderment. He was full of fear. Then the terror began to fade, to be replaced by an exhaustion which had something of contentment in it.

'*Now I have flesh again. Now I have flesh,*' said a pathetic voice.

And it was the barbarian Ashnar, his face all ruined, his eyes all crazy. He had dropped his sword and had not noticed. He kept touching himself, digging at his face with his nails. And he giggled.

John ap-Rhyss raised his head from the floor. He looked at Hawkmoon in hatred, then he looked away again. Emshon of Ariso, his sword, too, forgotten, crawled forward to help John ap-Rhyss rise to his feet. There was a cold silence in the manner of both men.

Others were mad or dead. Elric was helping Brut of

Lashmar up.

'What did you see?' asked the albino.

'More than I deserved, for all my sins. We were trapped – trapped in that skull . . .' The Knight of Lashmar broke down, his sobbing that of a little child. Elric held Brut, stroking his blond hair, unable to say anything which might ease the burden of his experience.

Erekosë murmured, almost to himself. 'We must go.' As he walked towards the door, his feet threatened to slide from under him.

'It was not fair,' said Hawkmoon to John ap-Rhyss and Emshon of Ariso, 'that you should suffer with us. It was not fair.'

John ap-Rhyss spat at the floor.

7

THE HEROES PART

Outside, standing amongst the shadows of buildings that were not there, or only partly standing; standing beneath a bloody sun which had not moved a fraction in the sky since they had landed on the island; Hawkmoon watched the bodies of the sorcerers burn.

The fire took eagerly, shrieking and howling as it consumed Agak and Gagak, and its smoke was whiter than Elric's face, redder than the sun. The smoke filled the sky.

Hawkmoon could remember little of what had befallen him inside Gagak's skull, but he was full of bitterness at that moment.

'I wonder if the Captain knew why he sent us here?' said Corum.

'Or if he suspected what would happen?' Hawkmoon wiped at his mouth.

'Only we – only that being – could battle Agak and Gagak in anything resembling their own terms.' Erekosë's eyes were full of a private knowledge. 'Other means would not have been successful. No other creature could have the particular qualities, the enormous power needed to slay such strange sorcerers.'

'So it seems,' said Elric. The albino had become taciturn, introspective.

Corum said encouragingly, 'Hopefully you will forget this experience as you forgot – or will forget – the other.'

Elric was not to be consoled. 'Hopefully, brother.'

Now Erekosë made an effort to break their mood. He chuckled. 'Who could recall that?'

Hawkmoon was bound to agree with him. Already the sensations were fading; already the experience had the feeling of an unusually powerful dream. He looked round at the soldiers who had fought with him; still none would meet his eye. Plainly they blamed him and his other manifestations for a horror they should not have had to confront. Ashnar the Lynx, tough-minded barbarian, was witness to the dreadful emotions they had had to suppress, to control, and now Ashnar gave out a chilling shriek and began to run towards the blaze. He ran until he had almost reached it and Hawkmoon thought he would throw himself upon the pyre, but he changed his direction at the last moment and ran instead into the ruins, swallowed by shadows.

'Why follow him?' said Elric. 'What can we do for him.' There was pain in his crimson eyes as he regarded the body of Hown Serpent-tamer, who had saved all their lives. Elric shrugged, but it was not a careless shrug. He shrugged as a man might who sought to adjust a particularly heavy load upon his shoulders.

John ap-Rhyss and Emshon of Ariso helped the dazed Brut of Lashmar to walk as they moved back from the fire, back towards the shore.

Hawkmoon said to Elric, as they walked. 'That sword of yours. It has a familiar look. It is no ordinary blade, eh?'

'No,' agreed the albino. 'It is not an ordinary blade, Duke Dorian. It is ancient, timeless, some say. Others think it was forged for my ancestors in a battle against gods. It has a twin, but that is lost.'

'I fear it,' said Hawkmoon. 'I know not why.'

'You are wise to fear it,' Elric told him. 'It is more than a sword.'

'A demon, too?'

'If you like.' Elric would say no more.

'It is the doom of the Champion to bear that blade at the Earth's most crucial crises,' Erekosë said. 'I have borne it and would not bear it again, if I had the choice.'

'The choice is rarely the Champion's,' Corum added

with a sigh.

Now they had come to the beach again and hovered there, contemplating the white mist surging on the water. The dark silhouette of the ship was plainly visible.

Corum, Elric and some of the others began to go forward into the mist, but Hawkmoon, Erekosë and Brut of Lashmar all hesitated at the same time. Hawkmoon had come to a decision.

'I will not rejoin the ship,' he said. 'I feel I've served my passage now. If I can find Tanelorn, this, I suspect, is where I must look.'

'My own feelings,' Erekosë moved his body so that he was looking again at the ruins.

Elric's glance at Corum was questioning and Corum smiled in answer.

'I have already found Tanelorn. I go back to the ship in the hope that soon it will deposit me upon a more familiar shore.'

'That is my hope.' Elric offered Brut, whom he supported, the same questioning stare.

Brut was whispering. Hawkmoon caught some of the words. 'What was it? What happened to us?'

'Nothing.' Elric gripped Brut's shoulder and then released it.

Brut broke free. 'I will stay. I am sorry.'

'Brut?' Elric frowned.

'I am sorry. I fear you. I fear that ship.' Brut stumbled backwards, stumbled inland.

'Brut?' Elric reached out a hand.

'Comrade,' said Corum, laying his silver hand upon Elric's own shoulder, 'let us be gone from this place. It is what is back there that I fear more than the ship.'

With one last moody look at the ruins, Elric said: 'With that I agree.'

'If that is Tanelorn, it is not, after all, the place I sought,' murmured Otto Blendker.

Hawkmoon expected John ap-Rhyss and Emshon of Ariso to go with Blendker, but they remained stolidly where they were.

'Will you stay with me?' said Hawkmoon in surprise.

The tall, long-haired man of Yel and the short, belligerent warrior of Ariso nodded together.

'We stay,' said John ap-Rhyss.

'You have no love for me, I thought.'

'You said that we suffered an injustice,' John ap-Rhyss told him. 'Well, that is true. It is not you we hate, Hawkmoon. It is those forces which control us all. I am glad that I am not Hawkmoon, yet I envy you in a way.'

'Envy?'

'I agree,' said Emshon soberly. 'To play such a role, one would give much.'

'One's soul?' said Erekosë.

'What is that?' asked John ap-Rhyss, refusing to meet the eye of the heavy-bodied man. 'A cargo we abandon too soon in our voyage, perhaps. Then we spend the rest of our lives trying to discover where we lost it.'

'Is that what you seek?' Emshon asked him.

John ap-Rhyss grinned a wolf's grin at him. 'Say so, if you wish.'

'Farewell to you, then,' said Corum, saluting them. 'We continue with the ship.'

'And I.' Elric drew his cloak about his face. 'I wish you success in your quest, brothers.'

'And you in yours,' said Erekosë. 'The Horn must be blown.'

'I do not understand you.' Elric's tone was cold. He turned and began to wade into the water, not waiting for an explanation.

Corum smiled. 'Removed from our times, plagued by paradoxes, manipulated by beings who refuse to enlighten us – it is tiresome, is it not?'

'Tiresome,' said Erekosë laconically. 'Aye.'

'My struggle has ended, I think,' said Corum. 'I believe that soon I will be allowed to die. I have served my turn as Champion Eternal. I join my Rhalina, my mortal bride.'

'I must still seek for my immortal Ermizhad,' said Erekosë.

'My Yisselda lives, I'm told,' Hawkmoon added. 'But I seek my children.'

'All the parts of the thing that is the Eternal Champion come together,' said Corum. 'This could be the last quest for all of us.'

'And shall we know peace, then?' Erekosë asked.

'Peace comes to a man only after he has struggled with himself,' said Corum. 'Is that not your experience?'

'It is the struggling which is so hard,' Hawkmoon told him.

Corum said no more. He followed Elric and Otto Blendker into the sea. Soon they had disappeared into the mist. Soon they heard faint shouts. Soon they heard the anchor raised. The ship was gone.

Hawkmoon was relieved, for all he did not relish the idea of what lay ahead of him. He turned.

The black figure was back. It was grinning at him. It was an evil, intimate grin.

'Sword,' it said. And it pointed after the ship. 'Sword. You will need me, Champion. Soon.'

Erekosë showed terror for the first time. Like Hawkmoon, his first instinct was to draw his blade, but something stopped him. John ap-Rhyss and Emshon of Ariso shouted in astonishment and Hawkmoon stayed their hands. 'Do not draw,' he said.

Brut of Lashmar merely stared at the apparition with his glazed, tired eyes.

'Sword,' said the creature. His black aura made it seem that he danced a peculiar, jerky jig, but his body was quite still. 'Elric? Corum? Hawkmoon? Erekosë? Urlik . . .?'

'Ah!' cried Erekosë. 'Now I know you. Go! Go!'

The black figure laughed. 'I can never go. Not while the Champion needs me.'

'The Champion needs you no longer,' said Hawkmoon, without knowing what he meant.

'He does! He does!'

'Go!'

The wicked face continued to grin.

'There are two of us now,' said Erekosë. 'Two are stronger.'

'But it is not allowed,' said the figure. 'It has never been allowed.'

'This is a different time, the Time of the Conjunction.'

'No!' cried the apparition.

Erekosë's laugh was contemptuous.

The black figure darted forward, became huge; darted back, became tiny; resumed its normal size, fled across the ruins, its own shadow capering behind it, not always in unison. The great, heavy shadows of that collection of cities seemed about to fall on the figure, for he recoiled from many of them.

'No!' they heard him cry. 'No!'

John ap-Rhyss said: 'Was that what was left of the sorcerer?'

'It was not,' said Erekosë. 'It is what is left of our nemesis.'

'You know it, then?' said Hawkmoon.

'I think so.'

'Tell me. It has haunted me since my adventure began. I think it was responsible for parting me from Yisselda, from my own world.'

'It has not the power for that, I'm sure,' said Erekosë. 'Doubtless, however, it was pleased to take advantage. I have only seen it once before, very briefly, in this manifestation.'

'What is it called?'

'Many names,' said Erekosë thoughtfully.

They began to move back into the ruins. The apparition had vanished again. Ahead they saw two new shadows; two huge shadows. They were the shadows of Agak and Gagak as they had looked when the heroes had first arrived here. The bodies had by this time burned to nothing. But the shadows remained.

'Tell me one?' Hawkmoon asked.

Erekosë pursed his lips before replying, then he darted a look directly into Hawkmoon's eyes. 'I think I understand why the Captain was reluctant to speculate, to divulge any information he could not be completely sure of. It is dangerous, in these circumstances, to jump to conclusions. Perhaps I am wrong, after all.'

'Oh!' cried Hawkmoon. 'Tell me what you suspect, then, Erekosë, if it is merely suspicion.'

'I think one of the names is Stormbringer,' the scarred man told him.

'And now I know why I feared Elric's sword,' Hawkmoon said.

They spoke no more of this.

BOOK THREE

IN WHICH MANY THINGS ARE FOUND TO BE ONE THING

1

PRISONERS IN SHADOWS

'We are like ghosts, are we not?'

Erekosë lay upon a pile of broken stones and stared up at the red, motionless sun. 'A converse of ghosts . . .' He smiled to show that he spoke idly, merely to pass time.

'I am hungry,' said Hawkmoon. 'That proves two things to me – that I'm made of ordinary flesh and that it has been a long while since our comrades returned to the ship.'

Erekosë sniffed at the cool air. 'Aye. I wonder, now, why I remained. Perhaps it is our fate to be marooned here – an irony, eh? Seeking Tanelorn we are allowed to exist in *all* the Tanelorns. Could this be all that remains?'

'I suspect not,' said Hawkmoon. 'Somewhere we'll find a gateway to the worlds we want.'

Hawkmoon sat on the shoulder of a fallen statue, trying to distinguish from the many shadows some shadow he might recognize.

Some yards away John ap-Rhyss and Emshon of Ariso were searching in the rubble for a box Emshon was sure he had seen on their way to do battle with Agak and Gagak and which, he had told John ap-Rhyss, was bound to contain something of value. Brut of Lashmar, a little better recovered, stood near them, not joining in the search.

Yet it was Brut who noticed later that a number of shadows which had previously been static were now in motion. 'Look, Hawkmoon,' he said. 'Is the city coming alive?'

The rest of the city remained as it had always been, but in one small corner of it, where the silhouette of a particularly ornate and delicate house was cast against the stained, white wall of a ruined temple, three or four of the human shadows were moving. And still they were only shadows – the men who cast them were not visible. It was like a play Hawkmoon had once witnessed, with puppets manipulated behind a screen.

Erekosë was on his feet, clambering towards the scene, Hawkmoon close at his heels and the others following a little less speedily.

And very faintly they could hear sounds – the clatter of weapons, shouts, the shuffle of booted feet on stone.

Erekosë stopped when his own height was almost equalled by the height of the shadows. Cautiously he reached out to touch one, stepping forward.

And Erekosë had vanished!

All that remained of him was his shadow. It had joined the others. Hawkmoon saw the shadow draw its sword and range itself beside another shadow, which seemed to him familiar. It was the shadow of a man no larger than Emshon of Ariso who watched the shadow-play with his mouth open, his eyes glazed.

Then the motion of the fighting men began to slow again. Hawkmoon was wondering how he might rescue Erekosë when the tall hero had reappeared, dragging another with him. The other shadows had frozen once more.

Erekosë was panting. The man with him was lacerated with a score of small wounds, but did not seem badly hurt. He was grinning in relief, wiping a whitish dust from the orange fur which covered his body, sheathing his sword, wiping his whiskers with the back of his paw-like hand. It was Oladahn. Oladahn of the Bulgar Mountains, kin to the Mountain Giants, Hawkmoon's closest friend and companion through most of his greatest adventures. Oladahn, who had died at Londra, who Hawkmoon had seen next as a glassy-eyed ghost in the swamps of the Kamarg and lastly upon the decks of *The Romanian Queen*, where, bravely, he had attacked Baron Kalan's crystal pyramid and, as a consequence, vanished.

'Hawkmoon!' Oladahn's joy at seeing his old comrade made him forget all else. He ran forward and embraced the Duke of Köln.

Hawkmoon found himself laughing with pleasure. He looked up at Erekosë. 'How you saved him I know not. But I am grateful to you.'

Erekosë, infected by their joy, laughed, too. 'How I saved him, I know not!' He glanced back at the static shadows. 'I found myself in a world scarcely more substantial than this one. I helped fight off those who attacked your friend – in desperation, as our movements became sluggish, I fell back – and here we are again!'

'How came you to that place, Oladahn?' Hawkmoon asked.

'My life has been confusing and my adventures peculiar since I last saw you aboard that ship,' Oladahn said. 'For a while I was the prisoner of Baron Kalan, unable to move my limbs, yet with my mind functioning normally. That was not pleasant. Then, suddenly, I was freed. I found myself upon a world involved in a battle between four or five different factions and served with one army and another, never quite understanding the issues involved. Then I was back in the Bulgar Mountains, wrestling a bear and getting the worst of the encounter. Then I came to a metal world, where I was the only creature of flesh amongst a motley variety of machines. About to be mangled by one of the machines (which was not without a certain philosophical intelligence) I was saved by Orland Fank – you remember him? – and taken to the world I have just escaped from. Fank and I sought the Runestaff there, a world of cities and of conflict. On an errand for Fank in a particularly violent quarter of one of the cities, I was set upon by more men than I could deal with. About to be slain, I found myself again frozen. This condition lasted for hours or for years (that I shall never know) until just before I was rescued by your comrade here. Tell me, Hawkmoon, what became of our other friends?'

'It's a long tale and it has little point, since I can explain few of the events in it,' Hawkmoon told him. He recounted something of his adventures, of Count Brass, Yisselda and his missing children, of the defeat of both Taragorm and Baron Kalan, of the disruption their insane vengeance and scheming had brought to the multiverse, ending: 'But of D'Averc and Bowgentle I can tell you nothing. They vanished much as you vanished. I would guess that their adventures are a match for yours. It is significant, is it not, that you have been snatched from inevitable death so many times?'

'Aye,' said Oladahn. 'I thought I had a supernatural protector – though I became tired of leaping, as it were, from the cooking pot into the stove! What have we here?' Stroking his whiskers, he looked about him, nodding politely to Brut, John and Emshon who were all staring at him in restrained amazement. 'It would seem significant that I have been allowed to join you again. But where is Fank?'

'I left him at Castle Brass, though he said nothing of meeting you. Doubtless he resumed his quest for the Runestaff and found you during that adventure.' Hawkmoon described everything he could of the nature of the island on which they now stood.

This description left Oladahn scratching at the red fur of his head, and shrugging his shoulders. Almost before Hawkmoon had finished, he was looking at the various rents in his jerkin and divided kilt, picking at the drying blood on his various wounds.

'Well, friend Hawkmoon,' he said, distracted, 'I'm content enough to be at your side again. Is there anything to eat?'

'Nothing,' John ap-Rhyss said feelingly. 'We'll starve to death if we can find no game on this island. And nothing appears to live here, save ourselves.'

As if in answer to this declaration, there came a howling from the other side of the city. They looked towards the source of the sound.

'A wolf?' Oladahn asked.

'A man, I think,' said Erekosë. He had not sheathed his sword and he used it to point.

Ashnar the Lynx came running towards them, leaping over stones, darting around tottering towers, his own sword raised above his head, his mad eyes glaring, the little bones in his braids dancing about his savage skull. Hawkmoon thought he attacked, but then he saw that Ashnar was pursued by a tall, lean, red-faced man in a bonnet and kilt, a plaid flying from his shoulders, his sword bouncing in the scabbard at his side.

'Orland Fank!' cried Oladahn. 'Why does he chase that man?'

Hawkmoon could hear Fank's shouts now. 'Come here, will ye? Come here, man! I mean ye no harm!'

Then Ashnar had tripped and fell, whimpering and scrabbling amongst dusty stones. Fank reached him, knocked the sword from his hand, gathered a fistful of braids and raised the barbarian's head.

Hawkmoon called: 'He is mad, Fank. Be gentle with him.'

Fank looked up. 'So it's Sir Hawkmoon, is it? And Oladahn? I wondered what had become of ye – deserted me, did you?'

'Almost,' answered the kin of the Mountain Giants feelingly, 'to Brother Death into whose arms you sent me, Master Fank.'

Fank grinned, letting go of Ashnar's hair.

The barbarian made no effort to rise, merely lay in the dust and moaned.

'What harm has that man offered you?' Erekosë asked Fank sternly.

'None. I could find no other human being in this gloomy conglomeration. I wanted to question him. When I approached him he let forth his heathen howling and tried to escape.'

'How found you this place?' Erekosë asked.

'By an accident. My quest for a certain artefact has led me through several of the Earth's many planes. I had heard that the Runestaff might be found in a certain city – called, by some, Tanelorn. I sought Tanelorn. My investigations led me to a sorcerer in a city on the world where I found young Oladahn here. The sorcerer was a man made all of metal and he was able to direct my path to the next plane, where Oladahn and I lost each other. I found a gateway and entered it and here I am . . .'

'Then let's make haste back to your gateway,' said Hawkmoon eagerly.

Orland Fank shook his head. 'Nay, it's closed behind me. Besides, I've no wish to return to that strifing world. Is this not, then, Tanelorn?'

'It is all the Tanelorns,' said Erekosë. 'Or so we think, Master Fank. Leastways, it is what remains of them. Was not the city you were in called Tanelorn?'

'Once,' said Fank. 'Or so a legend said. But men came who made selfish use of its properties and Tanelorn died, to be replaced by its opposite.'

'So Tanelorn can die?' Brut of Lashmar looked miserable. 'It is not invulnerable . . .'

'Only if those who dwell in it are men who have lost that particular kind of pride which destroys love – so I heard, at any rate.' Orland Fank looked embarrassed. 'And are therefore themselves invulnerable.'

'Any city would be preferable to this dumping ground of lost ideals,' said Emshon of Ariso, showing that while he had taken Orland Fank's point he was not particularly impressed by it. The dwarfish warrior tugged at his moustaches and grumbled on to himself for a while.

110

'So these would be all the "failures",' said Erekosë. 'We stand amongst the ruins of Hope. A wasteland of broken faith.'

'So I would surmise,' Fank replied. 'But nonetheless there must be a way through to a Tanelorn which has not succumbed, where the borderline is narrow. And that is what we must seek for now.'

'But how do we know what to seek?' John ap-Rhyss asked reasonably.

'The answer lies within ourselves,' Brut said in a voice that was not really his. 'That is what I was once told. Look for Tanelorn within yourself – an old woman said that when I asked her where I might find that fabulous city and know peace. I dismissed the statement as being empty of any real meaning, merely a piece of philosophical obfuscation, but I begin to realize that she offered me practical advice. Hope is what we have lost, gentlemen, and Tanelorn will open her gates only to those who hope. Faith flees from us, but faith is required before we can see the Tanelorn we need.'

'I think you speak good sense, Brut of Lashmar,' said Erekosë. 'For all that, of late, I have come to adopt the soldier's armour of cynicism, I understand you. But how can mortals hope in a sphere dominated by bickering gods, by the warring of those they desire so much to respect?'

'When gods die, self-respect buds,' murmured Orland Fank. 'Gods and their examples are not needed by those who respect themselves and, consequently, respect others. Gods are for children, for little, fearful people, for those who would have no responsibility to themselves or their fellows.'

'Aye!' John ap-Rhyss's melancholy features were almost cheerful.

A mood was coming to them all. They laughed as they looked from face to face.

And then Hawkmoon was drawing out his sword and

pointing it upward, towards the stagnant sun, and he cried:

'Here's Death for gods and Life for men! Let the Lords of Chaos and of Law destroy themselves in pointless conflict. Let the Cosmic Balance swing how it likes, it shall not affect out destinies.'

'It shall not!' shouted Erekosë, his own sword raised. 'It shall not!'

And John ap-Rhyss, and Emshon of Ariso, and Brut of Lashmar all drew their swords and echoed the cry.

Only Orland Fank seemed reluctant. He tugged at his clothing. He fingered his face.

And when they had done with their impetuous ceremony, the Orkneyman said:

'Then none of you will help me seek the Runestaff?'

And a voice from behind Orland Fank said:

'Father, you need seek no further.'

And there sat the child whom Hawkmoon had seen in Dnark, who had transformed himself into pure energy in order to inhabit the Runestaff when Shenegar Trott, Count of Sussex, had sought to steal it. The one who had been called the Spirit of the Runestaff, Jehamiah Cohnahlias. The boy's smile was radiant, his manner friendly.

'Greetings to you all,' he said. 'You summoned the Runestaff.'

'We did not summon it,' said Hawkmoon.

'Your hearts summoned it. And now, here is your Tanelorn.'

The boy spread his hands and it seemed as he spread them that the city became transformed. Rainbow light filled the sky. The sun shuddered and burned golden. Pinnacles, seeming slender as needles, raised themselves into the glowing air, and colours gleamed, pure and translucent, and a great stillness came upon that city, the stillness of tranquillity.

'Here is your Tanelorn.'

2

IN TANELORN

'Come, I will show you some history,' said the child.

And he led the men through quiet streets where people greeted them with friendly gravity.

If the city shone, now, it shone with a light so subtle that it was impossible to identify its source. If it had one colour, it was a kind of whiteness which certain kinds of jade have, but as white contains all colours, the city was of all colours. It thrived; it was happy; it was at peace. Families lived here; artists and craftsmen worked here; books were written; it was vital. This was no pallid harmony – the false peace of those who deny the body its pleasures, the mind its stimuli. This was Tanelorn.

This, at last, was Tanelorn, perhaps the model for so many other Tanelorns.

'We are at the centre,' said the child, 'the still, unalterable centre of the multiverse.'

'What gods are worshipped here?' asked Brut of Lashmar, his voice and his face relaxed.

'No gods,' said the child. 'They are not required.'

'And is that why they are said to hate Tanelorn?' Hawkmoon stepped to one side to allow a very old woman to pass him.

'It could be,' said the child. 'For the proud cannot accept being ignored. They have a different sort of pride in Tanelorn – and that is a pride which prefers to be ignored.'

He took them past high towers and lovely battlements, through parks where excited children played.

'They play at war, then, even here?' said John ap-Rhyss.
'Even here!'

'It is how children learn,' said Jehamiah Cohnahlias. 'And if they learn properly, they learn enough to abjure warfare when they are grown.'

'But the gods play at war,' said Oladahn.

'They are children, then,' said the child.

Hawkmoon noticed that Orland Fank was weeping, but he did not seem to be sad.

They came to a cleared part of the city, a kind of amphitheatre, but its sides consisted of three ranks of statues, somewhat larger than life size. All the statues were of the same colouring as the city; all seemed to glow with something resembling life. All the first rank of statues were of warriors, the second rank was chiefly of warriors, too, and the third rank was of women. There seemed to be thousands of these statues, in a great circle, beneath a sun which hung above the centre, red and still, as it had been on the island – but the red was mellow, the sky a warm, faded blue. It was as if it were evening here, always.

'Behold,' said the child. 'Behold Hawkmoon, Erekosë. These are you.' And he lifted one of his arms in its heavy, golden sleeve, to point at the first rank of statues, and there was a dull, black staff in his hand which Hawkmoon recognized as the Runestaff. And he noticed, for the first time, that the runes carved on it were in a script not dissimilar to that which was carved into the sword which Elric had borne, the Black Sword, Stormbringer.

'Look on their faces,' said the child. 'Look Erekosë, look Hawkmoon, look Champion Eternal.'

Looking, Hawkmoon saw faces he recognized amongst the statues. He saw Corum and he saw Elric and he heard Erekosë murmur: 'John Daker, Urlik Skarsol, Asquiol, Aubec, Arflane, Valadek . . . They are all here . . . all, save Erekosë . . .'

'And Hawkmoon,' said Hawkmoon.

Orland Fank spoke. 'There are gaps in the ranks. Why

114

so?'

'They wait to be filled,' said the child.

Hawkmoon shivered.

'They are all the manifestations of the Champion Eternal,' said Orland Fank. 'Their comrades, their consorts. All in one place. Why are we here, Jehamiah?'

'Because the Runestaff has summoned us.'

'I'll serve it no longer!' This was Hawkmoon. 'It has done me much harm.'

'You need not serve it, save in one way,' said the child mildly. 'It serves you. You summoned it.'

'I tell you that we did not.'

'And I told you that your hearts summoned it. You found the gateway to Tanelorn, you opened it, you allowed me to reach you.'

'This is mystical maundering of the most outrageous kind!' Emshon of Ariso bristled. He made to turn away.

'It is the truth, however,' said the child. 'Faith bloomed within you when you stood in those ruins. Not Faith in an ideal, or in gods, or the fate of the world – but Faith in yourselves. It is a force to defeat every enemy. It was the only force which could summon the friend that I am to you.'

'But this is a business concerning heroes,' said Brut of Lashmar. 'I am not a hero, boy, not as these two are.'

'That is for you to decide, of course.'

'I'm a plain soldier, a man of many faults . . .' began John ap-Rhyss. He sighed. 'I sought only rest.'

'And you have found it. You have found Tanelorn. Do you not, however, wish to witness the outcome of your ordeal upon the island?'

John ap-Rhyss directed a quizzical glance at the child. He tugged at his nose. 'Well . . .'

'It is the least you deserve. No harm will come to you, warrior.'

115

John ap-Rhyss shrugged and his shrug was imitated by Emshon and Brut.

'That ordeal? Was it connected with our quest?' Hawkmoon was eager. 'Was there some other point to it?'

'It was the Eternal Champion's last great deed for humanity. It has come full circle, Erekosë. You understand my meaning?'

Erekosë bowed his head. 'I do.'

'And the time is coming,' said the child, 'for the last deed of all – the deed which will free you from your curse.'

'Free?'

'Freedom, Erekosë, for the Champion Eternal and all those he has served down the long ages.'

Erekosë's face filled with dawning hope.

'But it has still to be earned,' cautioned the Spirit of the Runestaff. 'Still.'

'How can I earn it?'

'That you will discover. Now – watch.'

The child motioned with his staff at the statue of Elric. And they watched.

3

THE DEATHS OF THE UNDYING

They watched as one statue stepped down from its dais, face blank, limbs stiff – and slowly his features assumed the qualities of flesh (though bone-white flesh) and his armour turned black and a real person stood there; and though the face was animated he did not see them.

The scene around him had altered profoundly. Hawkmoon felt something in himself drawing him closer and closer to the one who had been a statue. It was as if their faces touched, and still the other was not aware of Hawkmoon's presence.

Then Hawkmoon was looking out of Elric's eyes. Hawkmoon was Elric. Erekosë was Elric.

He was tugging the black sword from the body of his greatest friend. He was sobbing as he tugged. At last the sword was dragged from the corpse and flung aside, landing with a strange, muffled sound. He saw the sword move, approaching him. It stopped, but it watched.

He placed a large horn to his lips and he took a deep breath. He had the strength to blow the horn now, whereas earlier he had been weak. Another's strength filled him.

He blew a note upon the horn; one great blast. Then there was silence upon the plain of rock. Silence waited in the high and distant mountains.

In the sky a shadow began to materialize. It was a vast shadow and then it was not a shadow at all but an outline, and then details filled the outline. It was a gigantic hand and in the hand was a balance, its scales swinging erratically. Now, however, the scales became steadier until, at length, the balance righted itself. The sight brought a certain relief to the grief he felt. He dropped the horn.

'There is something, at least,' he heard himself say, 'and if it's an illusion, then it's a reassuring one.'

But now, as he turned, he saw that the sword had risen into the air of its own volition. It menaced him.

'STORMBRINGER!'

The blade entered his body, entered his heart. The blade drank his soul. Tears fell from his eyes as the sword drank; he knew that part of him, now, would never have peace.

He died.

He fell away from his fallen body and he was Hawkmoon again. He was Erekosë again . . .

The two aspects of the same thing watched as the sword pulled itself free from the body of the last of the Bright Emperors. They watched as the sword began to change its shape (though a husk of the blade remained and became human in proportions, standing over the man it had conquered).

The being was the same Hawkmoon had seen on the Silver Bridge, the same he had seen on the island. It smiled.

'Farewell, friend,' said the being. 'I was a thousand times more evil than thou!'

It flung itself into the sky, laughing, malicious, without kindness. It mocked the Cosmic Balance, its ancient enemy.

And it was gone, and the scene was gone, and the statue of the Prince of Melniboné stood again upon its dais.

Hawkmoon was gasping as if he had escaped drowning. His heart was beating horribly.

He saw that Oladahn's face twitched and that his eyes held shock; he saw Erekosë's frowning countenance, and he saw Orland Fank rubbing at his jaw. He saw the serene face of the child. He saw John ap-Rhyss, Emshon of Ariso and Brut of Lashmar, and he knew, when he looked at them, that they had witnessed nothing in the scene which had disturbed them.

'So it is confirmed,' said Erekosë's deep voice. 'That

118

thing and the sword are the same.'

'Often,' said the child. 'Sometimes its whole spirit does not inhabit the sword. Kanajana was not the whole sword.'

The child motioned. 'Watch again.'

'No,' said Hawkmoon.

'Watch again,' said the child.

Another tall statue stepped from its place.

The man was handsome and he had only one eye; only one hand. He had known love and he had known grief and the love had taught him how to bear the grief. His features were calm. Somewhere, the sea crashed. He had come home.

Again Hawkmoon felt himself absorbed and knew that Erekosë, too, was absorbed. Corum Jhaelen Irsei, Prince in the Scarlet Robe, Last of the Vadhagh, who had refused to fear beauty and who had fallen to it, who had refused to fear a brother and had been betrayed, who had refused to fear a harp and had been slain by it, who had been banished from a place where he did not belong, had come home.

He emerged from a forest and stood upon a seashore. The tide would be out soon and it would uncover the causeway leading to Moidel's Mount where he had been happy with a woman of the short-lived Mabden race, who had died and left him desolate (for children rarely come from such a union).

The memory of Medhbh was fading, but the memory of Rhalina, Margravine of the East, could not fade.

The causeway appeared and he began to walk across. The castle on Moidel's Mount was deserted now, that was plain. It showed neglect. A wind whispered through the towers, but it was a friendly wind.

On the other side of the causeway, standing in the entrance to the castle courtyard, he saw one he recognized – a nightmare creature, greenish blue in colour, with four squat legs, four brawny arms, a barbaric, noseless head with the nostrils set directly into the face, a wide, grinning mouth, full of sharp teeth, eyes that were faceted like a fly's. There were swords of strange design at its belt. It was the Lost God: Kwll.

'Greetings, Corum.'

'Greetings, Kwll, slayer of gods. Where is your brother?' He was pleased to see his old, reluctant, ally.

'At his own devices. We grow bored and ready to leave the multiverse. There is no place for us in it, as there is no place for you.'

'So I have been told.'

'We go on one of our journeys, at least until the time of the next Conjunction.' Kwll gestured at the sky. 'We must make haste.'

'Where do you go?'

'There is another place – a place deserted by those you destroyed here – a place where they still have use for gods. Would Corum come with us? The Champion must remain, but Corum can come.'

'Are they not the same?'

'They are the same. But that which is not the same, that which is Corum only, he can come with us. It is an adventure.'

'I weary of adventures, Kwll.'

The Lost God grinned. 'Consider. We need a mascot. We need the strength you have.'

'What strength is that?'

'The strength of Man.'

'All gods need that, do they not?'

'Aye,' Kwll agreed, somewhat reluctantly, 'but some need it more than others. Rhynn and Kwll have Kwll and Rhynn, but it would amuse us if you came.'

Corum shook his head.

'You understand that you cannot live after the Conjunction?'

'I understand that, Kwll.'

'And you know now, I suppose, that it was not I who actually destroyed the Lords of Law and Chaos?'

'I think so.'

120

'I merely finished the work you had begun, Corum.'

'You are kind.'

'I speak the truth. I am a boastful god, having no loyalties, save to Rhynn. But I am, by and large, a truthful god. Departing, I leave you with the truth.'

'Thank you, Kwll.'

'Farewell.' The barbaric figure vanished.

Corum walked through the courtyard, through the dusty halls and corridors of the castle, up to the high tower where he could look across the sea. And he knew that Lwym-an-Esh, that lovely land, was now drowned, that only a few fragments still stood above the waves. And he sighed, but he was not unhappy.

He saw a black figure come capering over the waves towards him, a grinning figure with an insinuating stare.

'Corum? Corum?'

'I know you,' said Corum.

'May I guest with you, Corum? There is much I can do for you. I would be your servant, Corum.'

'I need no servant.'

The figure stood upon the sea, swaying with the movements of the waves.

'Let me into your castle, Corum.'

'I require no guests.'

'I can bring your loved ones to you.'

'They are already with me.' And Corum stood upon the battlements, laughing down at the black figure, who glowered and sneered. And Corum jumped so that his body would strike the rocks at the foot of Moidel's Mount, so that his spirit would be freed from it.

And the black figure bellowed with rage, with frustration and, finally, with fear . . .

'That is the last creature of Chaos, is it not?' said Erekosë when the scene had faded and the statue of Corum resumed its place.

121

'In that guise,' said the child, 'it is, poor thing.'

'I have known it so many times,' said Erekosë. 'It has sometimes worked for good . . .'

'Chaos is not wholly evil, surely?' said the child. 'And neither is Law wholly good. They are primitive divisions, at best – they represent only temperamental preferences in individual men and women. There are other elements . . .'

'You speak of the Cosmic Balance?' said Hawkmoon. 'Of the Runestaff?'

'Call that Conscience, eh?' said Orland Fank. 'But can you call it Tolerance?'

'All are primitive,' said the child.

'You would admit that?' Oladahn was surprised. 'Then what would replace them that would be better?'

The child smiled, but would not reply.

'Would you see more?' he asked Hawkmoon and Erekosë. They shook their heads.

'That black figure daunts us always,' said Hawkmoon. 'It plots our destruction.'

'It needs your souls,' said the child.

John ap-Rhyss said calmly, 'In Yel, in the villages, they have a legend of such a creature. Say-tunn, is that his name?'

The child shrugged. 'Give him any name and he grows in power. Refuse him a name and his power weakens. I call him Fear. Mankind's greatest enemy.'

'But a good friend to those who would use him,' said Emshon of Ariso.

Oladahn said: 'For a time.'

'A treacherous friend, even to those he helps most,' said the child. 'Oh, how he longs to be admitted to Tanelorn.'

'He cannot enter?'

'Only at this time, because he comes to barter.'

'In what does he trade?' Hawkmoon asked.

'In souls, as I said. In souls. Look, I will admit him.'

And the child seemed perturbed as he motioned with his staff. 'He travels, now, from Limbo.'

4

CAPTIVES OF THE SWORD

'I am the Sword,' said the black figure. He waved a hand airily at the massed statues all around them. 'These were mine once. I owned the multiverse.'

'You have been disinherited,' said the child.

'By you?' the black figure smiled.

'No,' said the child. 'We share a fate, as you well know.'

'You cannot give me back the things I must have,' said the figure. 'Where is it?' He looked about him. 'Where?'

'I have not yet summoned it. Where are . . .?'

'My bartering goods? Those I shall summon when I know that you have what I need.' He grinned a greeting at Hawkmoon and Erekosë, saying carelessly, to nobody in particular, 'I gather that all the gods are dead.'

'Two have fled,' said the child. 'The rest are dead.'

'So only we remain.'

'Aye,' said the child. 'The sword and the staff.'

'Created at the beginning,' said Orland Fank, 'after the last Conjunction.'

'Few mortals know that,' said the black figure. 'My body was made to serve Chaos, his to serve the Balance, others to serve Law, but all those are gone now.'

'What replaces them?' said Erekosë.

'That remains to be decided,' said the black figure. 'I come to barter for that body of mine. Either manifestation will do; or both.'

'You are the Black Sword?'

The child motioned again with the staff. Jhary-a-Conel stood there, his hat at an angle, his cat on his shoulder. At Oladahn he stared with particular bemusement. 'Should we both be here?'

Oladahn said: 'I do not know you, sir.'

'Then you do not know yourself, sir.' Jhary bowed to Hawkmoon. 'Greetings. I believe this is yours, Duke Dorian.' He held something in his hands and was moving forward to offer it to Hawkmoon when the child said:

'Stay! Show him.'

Jhary-a-Conel paused somewhat theatrically, eyeing the black figure. 'Show him? Must I? The mewler?'

'Show me,' whispered the black figure. 'Please, Jhary-a-Conel.'

Jhary-a-Conel rubbed at the head of the child, as an uncle might greet a favourite nephew. 'How fare you, cousin?'

'Show him,' said the child.

Jhary-a-Conel put one hand on the pommel of his sword, stuck out his leg, stuck out his elbow, looked thoughtfully at the black figure, then, with a sudden, conjurer's gesture, presented that which lay in his palm.

The black figure hissed. His eyes glowed.

'The Black Jewel!' gasped Hawkmoon. 'You have the Black Jewel.'

'The Jewel will do,' said the figure eagerly. 'Here . . .'

Two men, two women and two children appeared. Golden chains held them; links of golden silk.

'I treat them well,' said the one who called himself Sword.

One of the men, tall, slender, languid of manner, dandified of dress, held up his shackled wrists. 'Oh,' he said, 'this luxury of chains!'

All but one of them did Hawkmoon recognize. And he was full of cold anger now. 'Yisselda! Yarmila and Manfred! D'Averc! Bowgentle! How are you this creature's prisoners.'

'That tale's a long one . . .' began Huillam D'Averc, but his voice was drowned by Erekosë and Erekosë was shouting with joy:

125

'Ermizhad! My Ermizhad!'

The woman, whom Hawkmoon had not recognized, was of a race resembling Elric's and Corum's. In her own way, she was as beautiful as Yisselda. There was much in the two women's very different faces which provoked a sense of resemblance.

Bowgentle turned an apparently placid face this way and that. 'So we are in Tanelorn at last.'

The woman called Ermizhad was straining at her chains, trying to reach Erekosë.

'I thought you Kalan's prisoners,' said Hawkmoon through the confusion, addressing D'Averc.

'I thought so, too, but I believe this somewhat demented gentleman intercepted our journey through Limbo . . .' D'Averc made a pantomime of dismay as Erekosë glared at the black figure.

'You must release her!'

The being smiled. 'I will have the jewel first. She and the others for the jewel. It was the bargain we made.'

Jhary-a-Conel clenched his fingers around the jewel. 'Why do you not take it from me? You claim power?'

'Only a Hero may give it to him,' said the child. 'He knows that.'

'Then I will give it to him,' said Erekosë.

'No,' said Hawkmoon. 'If anyone has the right, I have it. Through the Black Jewel I was made a slave. Now, at least, I can use it to free those I love.'

The expression on the black being's face became eager. 'Not yet,' said the child.

Hawkmoon ignored him. 'Give me the Black Jewel, Jhary.'

Jhary-a-Conel looked first at the one he had addressed as 'cousin', then at Hawkmoon. He hesitated.

'That jewel,' said the child quietly, 'is one aspect of one of the two most powerful things at present existing in the multiverse.'

'And the other?' said Erekosë, looking yearningly at the woman he had sought for through eternity.

'The other is this, the Runestaff.'

'If the Black Jewel is Fear, then what is the Runestaff?' asked Hawkmoon.

'Justice,' said the child, 'the enemy of Fear.'

'If you both hold so much power,' Oladahn said reasonably, 'then why are we involved?'

'Because neither can exist without Man,' said Orland Fank. 'They go with Man wherever He goes.'

'That is why you are here,' said the child. 'We are your creations.'

'Yet you control our destinies.' Erekosë's eyes had never left Ermizhad's. 'How?'

'Because you let us,' the child told him.

'Well, then, "Justice", let me see you keep your word,' said the creature called Sword.

'My word was given that I would admit you to Tanelorn,' said the child. 'I can do no more. The bargain itself must be debated with Hawkmoon and Erekosë.'

'The Black Jewel for your captives? Is that the bargain?' Hawkmoon said. 'What will the jewel give you?'

'It will give him back some of the power he lost during the war between the gods,' said the child. 'And that power will enable him to bring more power for himself and pass easily into the new multiverse which will exist after the Conjunction.'

'Power which will serve you well,' said the black figure to Hawkmoon.

'Power we have never wished for,' said Erekosë.

'What do *we* lose if we agree?' Hawkmoon said.

'You lose my help, almost certainly.'

'Why is that?'

'I shall not say.'

'Mysteries!' said Hawkmoon. 'Discretion sadly misguided in my opinion, Jehamiah Cohnahlias.'

'I say nothing because I respect you,' said the child. 'But if the opportunity should come, then use the staff to smash the jewel.'

Hawkmoon took the Black Jewel from Jhary's hand. It was lifeless, without the familiar pulse, and he knew it was lifeless because that which inhabited it now stood before him in another guise.

'So,' said Hawkmoon, 'this is your home.'

He reached towards the creature, the Black Jewel upon the palm of his hand.

The chains of golden silk fell away from the limbs of the six captives.

Laughing, confident, his eyes glowing with evil triumph, the being took the Black Jewel from Hawkmoon's hand.

Hawkmoon embraced his children. He kissed his daughter. He kissed his son.

Erekosë held Ermizhad in his arms and he could not speak.

And the Spirit of the Black Jewel raised his prize to his lips.

And he swallowed the jewel.

'Take this,' said the child urgently to Hawkmoon. 'Quickly.' He handed Hawkmoon the Runestaff.

The black being shrieked his glee. 'I am myself again! I am more than myself again!'

Hawkmoon kissed Yisselda of Brass.

'*I am myself again!*'

When Hawkmoon looked up, the Spirit of the Black Jewel had vanished.

Hawkmoon turned with a smile to remark on this to the child, Jehamiah Cohnahlias. The child had his back to Hawkmoon at that moment, but his head was turning.

'I have won,' said the child.

His face had turned completely. Hawkmoon thought his

heart would stop. He felt faint.

The face of the child was still its own, but it had changed. Now it glowed with a dark aura. Now it grinned with an unholy joy. It was the face of the creature which had swallowed the Black Jewel. It was the face of Sword.

'I have won!'

And the child began to giggle.

And then it began to grow.

It grew until it was the size of one of the statues surrounding the group. Its garments shredded and fell away and it was a man, dark and naked, with a red mouth full of fangs, with a yellow, glaring eye, with a presence which radiated immense and terrifying power.

'I HAVE WON!'

He cast about him, ignoring the party.

'Sword,' he said. 'Now, where is the sword?'

'It is here,' said a new voice. 'I have it here. Can you see me?'

5

THE CAPTAIN AND THE STEERSMAN

'It was found on the Southern Ice, at sunrise, after you had but recently left that world, Erekosë. It had performed one action for humanity which was not directly to its benefit and so its spirit was driven from it.'

The Captain stood there, his blind eyes staring beyond them. Next to him was his twin, the steersman, with arms outstretched, the great black runesword held on the flats of both palms.

'It was that manifestation of the sword that we sought,' continued the Captain. 'It was a long quest for us and it lost us our ship.'

'But surely,' said Erekosë, 'so little time has passed since we left you?'

The Captain smiled ironically. 'There is no such thing as time,' he said, 'particularly in Tanelorn, particularly at the Conjunction of the Million Spheres. If time existed, as men consider it, then how can you and Hawkmoon exist here together?'

Erekosë made no reply; he hugged his Eldren princess closer to him.

The being roared. 'GIVE ME THE SWORD!'

'I cannot,' said the Captain, 'as you well know. And you cannot take it. You can only inhabit (or be inhabited by) one of the two manifestations, sword or jewel. Never both.'

The being snarled, but it made no movement towards the Black Sword.

Hawkmoon looked at the staff the child had given him and he saw that he had been right, the runes in the staff corresponded in some manner to those on the sword. He addressed the Captain.

'Who made these artefacts?'

'The smiths who forged this sword long ago, close to the beginning of the Great Cycle, required a spirit to inhabit it to give it power above all other weapons. They struck a bargain with this spirit (whom we shall not name).' The Captain turned his blind head so that it faced the black creature. 'You were glad to accept it, then. Two swords were forged and part of you went into each, but one of the swords was destroyed, so you inhabited the whole of the remaining blade. The smiths who forged the swords were not human, but they worked for humanity. They sought to fight Chaos, at that time, for they were loyal to the Lords of Law. They thought they used Chaos to conquer Chaos. They learned the flaws in that belief . . .'

'They did!' The creature grinned. 'Oh, they did!'

'So they made the Runestaff and they sought the aid of your brother, who served Law. They did not realize that you and he are not really brothers at all, but aspects of the same single being, now united again, but infused with the power of the Black Jewel, with your own dark power magnified. A seeming paradox . . .'

'A paradox I find most useful,' said the black being.

The Captain ignored him, continuing: 'They made the jewel in an effort to trap you, to imprison you. It gave the jewel great power, it held the souls of others as well as your own, just as the sword did, but you could be released from the jewel just as sometimes you could be released from the sword . . .'

' "Banished" is a better word,' said the creature, 'for I love my body, the sword. There will always be men to bear me as a sword.'

'Not always,' said the Captain. 'The Cosmic Balance was the last great artefact created by these smiths before they returned to their own worlds – a symbol of Equilibrium between Law and Chaos, it had a power of its own, incorporated into the Runestaff – to produce Order between Law and Chaos. And it is that which checks even you, at this moment.'

'Not when I have the Black Sword!'

'You have tried for so long to assume complete domination of mankind, and sometimes, for a while, you have almost achieved it. The Conjunction takes place on many different worlds, in many different eras, the manifestations of the Champion Eternal perform their great deeds, to rid the multiverse of the gods their forebears' desires created. And, in a world free of gods, you can retain the power you have been greedy for through the ages. You slew Elric in one world; you slew the Silver Queen in another, you sought to slay Corum, you have slain more who thought you served them. But Elric's death set you free and the death of the Silver Queen brought life to the Earth when it was dying (your own interests were served, but the interest of mankind was, at last, served better). You could not get your "body" back. You felt your power waning. The experiments of two insane sorcerers on Hawkmoon's world induced a situation which you could exploit. You need the Champion Eternal, that is your fate, but he no longer needs you, so you had to gather captives and bargain with the Champion with those he loves. Now you have the power of the jewel and you have taken over the body of your brother, who was once Orland Fank's son. Now you would smash the Balance, but you know that in destroying the Balance you will be destroyed yourself. Unless you have a refuge – a new body into which your spirit can escape.'

The Captain turned his head so that his sightless eyes seemed to regard Hawkmoon and Erekosë.

'Moreover,' he said, 'the sword must be wielded by a manifestation of the Champion, and here are two such manifestations. How will you induce one of them to serve your purpose?'

Hawkmoon looked at Erekosë. He said: 'My loyalties were ever to the Runestaff, though I resented giving them, at times.'

'And if I had loyalties, they were to the Black Sword,' said Erekosë.

'Which one of you will bear the Black Sword, then?' said the creature eagerly.

'Neither has to bear it,' the Captain told them quickly.

'But I now have the power to destroy all here,' said the creature.

'All save the two aspects of the Champion Eternal,' said the Captain, 'and my brother and myself, you cannot harm us.'

'I will destroy Ermizhad, Yisselda, the children – these others. I will eat them. I will have their souls.' The black being opened his red mouth wide and he reached a hand of black radiance towards Yarmila. The girl stared bravely back, but she was shrinking from him.

'And what will happen to us after you have destroyed the Balance?' asked Hawkmoon.

'Nothing,' said the being. 'You can live out your lives in Tanelorn. Even I cannot destroy Tanelorn, though the rest of the multiverse shall be mine.'

'It is true, what he says,' said the Captain. 'And he will keep his word.'

'But all humanity will suffer, save those in Tanelorn,' said Hawkmoon.

'Aye,' said the Captain, 'we shall all suffer, save you.'

'Then he must not be given the sword,' Hawkmoon said firmly, and he could not look at those he loved.

'Humanity suffers already,' Erekosë said. 'I have sought Ermizhad through eternity. I deserve this. I have served humanity through eternity, save once. I have suffered too long.'

'Would you repeat a crime?' asked the Captain quietly.

Erekosë ignored him, staring meaningfully at

Hawkmoon. 'The power of the Black Sword and the power of the Balance are equal at this moment, you say, Captain.'

'That's so.'

'And this being can inhabit either the sword or the jewel, not both?'

And Hawkmoon understood the implication of Erekosë's questions and kept his face expressionless.

'Hurry!' said the black being from behind them. 'Hurry. The Balance materializes!'

For an instant, Hawkmoon felt something of the experience that he had had when they had fought Agak and Gagak together, a oneness with Erekosë, sharing his emotions and his thoughts.

'Hurry, Erekosë,' said the being. 'Take the sword!'

Erekosë turned his back on Hawkmoon, staring up into the sky.

The Cosmic Balance hung, shining, in the sky, its scales in perfect equilibrium. It hung over that great concourse of statues, over every manifestation of the Eternal Champion there had ever been, over every woman he had ever loved, over every companion he had ever had. And, at that moment, it appeared to menace them all.

Erekosë took three paces until he stood before the steersman. There was no expression on the face of either man.

'Give me the Black Sword,' said the Eternal Champion.

6

THE SWORD AND THE STAFF

Erekosë placed one large hand upon the hilt of the Black Sword and he placed the other under the blade, lifting it from the steersman's grasp.

'Ah!' cried the creature. 'We are united!'

And he flowed towards the Black Sword and he laughed as he entered it, and the sword began to pulse, to sing, to emanate black fire, and the creature was gone.

But, Hawkmoon noticed, the Black Jewel had returned. He saw Jhary-a-Conel stoop and pick it up.

Now Erekosë's face glowed with a light of its own – a light of violence, of battle joy. His voice was a vibrating roar, a snarl of triumph. His eyes were alive with blood lust as he held the sword in two hands over his head, staring up at its long blade.

'At last!' he shouted. 'Erekosë shall have revenge on that which has manipulated his fate for so long! I will destroy the Cosmic Balance. With the Black Sword I will make amends for all the agony I have suffered through all the long ages of the multiverse! No longer do I serve humanity. Now I serve only the sword. Thus I shall be released from the bondage of aeons!'

And the sword moaned and writhed and its black radiance fell upon Erekosë's warrior's face and was reflected in his battle-mad eyes.

'Now, I destroy the Balance!'

And the sword seemed to pull Erekosë from the ground, up into the sky, up towards where the Balance hung, serene, apparently invulnerable, and Erekosë, Champion Eternal, had become huge and the sword blotted the light from the land.

Hawkmoon continued to watch, but he said to Jhary-a-Conel, 'Jhary – the jewel – place it before me on the ground.'

And Erekosë drew back his two arms to strike his blow. And he struck once.

There came a sound as if ten million large bells rang at once, a shattering noise as if the very cosmos cracked apart, and the Black Sword cut through the links holding one of the scales and it began to fall, the other scale rising higher, the beam swinging rapidly on its axis.

And the world shuddered.

The vast circle of statues trembled and threatened to tumble to the ground, and all who watched gasped.

And somewhere, something fell and broke into invisible fragments.

They heard laughter from the sky, but it was impossible to tell if the sword or the man who bore it was the source.

Erekosë, huge and dreadful, drew back his arms for the second stroke.

The sword swept through the sky and lightning flashed, thunder growled. It cut into the chains holding the other scale and that, too, fell.

And again the world shuddered.

And the Captain whispered: 'You have rid the world of gods, but now you rid it of order, too.'

'Only of Authority,' said Hawkmoon.

The steersman looked at him with intelligence, with interest.

Hawkmoon looked at the ground where the Black Jewel lay, dull, without life. Then he looked at the sky as Erekosë struck his third and final blow, struck at the central staff of the ruined Balance.

And light broke from the shattered remains and a strange, near-human howling reverberated through the world, and they were blinded and they were deafened.

But Hawkmoon heard the single word he waited for. He heard Erekosë's giant's voice call:

'NOW!'

And suddenly, the Runestaff was throbbing with life, in Hawkmoon's right hand, and the Black Jewel began to pulse, and Hawkmoon raised his arm for a single, powerful blow, the only blow which would be allowed him.

And he brought the Runestaff down with all his might upon the pulsing jewel.

And the jewel shattered and it shouted and it moaned in outrage, and the staff shattered, too, in Hawkmoon's hand, and the dark light bursting from the one met with the golden light bursting from the other. There came a screaming, a wailing, a whimper, and finally the whimper died, and a ball of red stuff hung before them, glowing only faintly, for the power of the Runestaff had cancelled out the power of the Black Sword. Then the red globe began to rise into the sky, higher and higher, until it hung directly over their heads.

And Hawkmoon was reminded of the star which had followed the Dark Ship on its voyage through the Seas of Limbo.

And then the red globe was absorbed into the warmer red of the sun itself.

The Black Jewel was gone. The Runestaff was gone. Destroyed, too, were the Black Sword and the Cosmic Balance. For a moment, their substance had sought refuge respectively in the jewel and the staff and it had been at that moment, when one destroyed the other, that Hawkmoon could use the other to destroy the one. It was what Erekosë had been able to agree with him just before he accepted the Black Sword.

And now something fell at Hawkmoon's feet.

Weeping, Ermizhad kneeled beside the corpse. 'Erekosë! Erekosë!'

'He has paid at last,' said Orland Fank. 'And at last he

rests. He found Tanelorn and he found you, Ermizhad –
and, finding them, he died for them.'

But Ermizhad did not hear Orland Fank, for she was
weeping; she was lost.

7

GOING BACK TO CASTLE BRASS

'The time of the Conjunction is almost passed,' said the Captain, 'and the multiverse begins another cycle. Free of gods, free of what you, Hawkmoon, might term "cosmic authority". Perhaps it will never need heroes again.'

'Only examples,' said Jhary-a-Conel. He was walking towards the statues, towards an empty space in the ranks. 'Farewell all of you. Farewell, Champion Who is no longer Champion, and farewell to you, in particular, Oladahn.'

'Where do you go, friend?' asked the kin of the Mountain Giants, scratching at the red fur of his head.

Jhary stopped and removed the little black and white cat from his shoulder. He pointed at the empty space amongst the statues. 'I go to take my place there. You live. I live. Farewell to you, for the very last time.'

And he stepped amongst the statues, and instantly he was a statue, cocky, smiling, pleased with himself.

'Is there a place for me there, too?' said Hawkmoon, turning to Orland Fank.'

'Not now,' said the Orkneyman, picking up Jhary-a-Conel's winged cat and stroking its back. It purred.

Ermizhad stood up and the tears were gone from her eyes. Saying nothing to the others, she, too, stepped into the ranks of the statues, finding another space. She raised her hand in a gesture of farewell, her flesh turned to the same pale colour of the surrounding statues and she stood frozen as they were frozen, and Hawkmoon saw that near her was another statue, the statue of Erekosë, who had sacrificed his life by taking up the Black Sword.

'Now,' said the Captain, 'would you and yours stay in

Tanelorn, Hawkmoon? You have earned the right.'

Hawkmoon put his arms around the shoulders of his children. He saw that there was happiness in them and he became happy. Yisselda put her hand to his cheek and smiled at him.

'No,' said Hawkmoon, 'we go back, I think, to Castle Brass. It is enough for us to know that Tanelorn exists. What of you, D'Averc? Oladahn? And you, Sir Bowgentle?'

'I have much to tell you, Hawkmoon, beside a good fire, with the good wine of the Kamarg in my hand, with good friends around me,' said Huillan D'Averc. 'At Castle Brass my tales would be of interest, but they would only bore the folk of Tanelorn. I'll come with you.'

'And I,' said Oladahn.

Bowgentle alone, seemed a little reluctant. He looked thoughtfully at the statues and back at the towers of Tanelorn. 'An interesting place. What created it, I wonder?'

'We created it,' said the Captain, 'my brother and I.'

'You?' Bowgentle smiled. 'I see.'

'And what is your name, sir?' Hawkmoon asked. 'You and your brother, what are you called?'

'We have only one name,' said the Captain.

And the steersman said: 'We are called Man.' He took his brother by the arm and began to lead him away from the circle of statues, back towards the city.

In silence, Hawkmoon, his family and his friends watched them go.

It was Orland Fank, clearing his throat, who broke the silence. 'I will stay, I think. My tasks are all completed. My quest is finished. I have seen my son come to peace of a kind. I will stay in Tanelorn.'

'Are there no gods left for you to serve?' asked Brut of Lashmar.

'Gods are but metaphors,' said Orland Fank. 'As

metaphors they might be very acceptable – but they should never be allowed to become beings in their own right.' Again he cleared his throat, seeming embarrassed by his next remark. 'The wine of poetry turns to poison when it becomes politics, eh?'

'You three are welcome to come to Castle Brass with us,' said Hawkmoon to the warriors.

Emshon of Ariso fiddled with his moustache and looked inquiringly at John ap-Rhyss who looked, in turn, at Brut of Lashmar.

'Our journey is over,' said Brut.

'We are but ordinary soldiers,' said John ap-Rhyss. 'No history will count us heroes. I stay in Tanelorn.'

'I began my life as a teacher in a school,' said Emshon of Ariso. 'It was never my dream to go warring. But there were indignities, inequalities, injustices and it seemed to me that only a sword could correct those things. I did my best. I have earned my peace. I, too, stay in Tanelorn. I would like to write a book, I think.'

Hawkmoon bowed his head in acknowledgement of their decision. 'I thank you, friends, for your help.'

'You would not stay with us?' said John ap-Rhyss. 'Have you not also earned the right to dwell here?'

'Perhaps, but I have a great liking for old Castle Brass, and I have left a friend there. Perhaps we can speak of what we know and show folk how to find Tanelorn within themselves.'

'Given the chance,' said Orland Fank, 'most find it. Only gods and the worship of fallacy, fear of their own humanity, blocks their path to Tanelorn.'

'Oh, I fear for my carefully manufactured personality!' laughed Huillam D'Averc. 'Is there anything duller than a reformed cynic?'

'Let Queen Flana decide that,' grinned Hawkmoon. 'Well, Orland Fank, we speak much of leaving – but how shall we leave now that there are no supernatural creatures to direct our destinies, now that the Champion is laid, at last, to rest?'

'I still have a little of my old power left,' said the Orkneyman, almost insulted. 'And it is easily used while the Spheres remain in Conjunction. And since it was partly my doing, and partly the doing of those seven you met in the unformed world of Limbo, it suits me to put you back upon your original journey.' His red face broke into a smile which was almost merry. 'Goodbye to ye all, Heroes of the Kamarg. Ye go to a world free of all authority. Be sure that the only authority you seek in future is the quiet authority which comes from self-respect.'

'You were ever a moralist, Orland Fank!' Bowgentle clapped his hand upon the Orkneyman's shoulder. 'But it is an art to make such simple morality work in a complicated world!'

'It is only the darkness of our own minds which makes for complications,' said Orland Fank. 'Good luck, too!' And he was laughing now, his bonnet bobbing on his head. 'Let us hope this is an end of tragedy.'

'And the beginning, perhaps, of comedy,' said Huillam D'Averc, smiling and shaking his head. 'Come – Count Brass awaits us!'

And they stood upon the Silver Bridge amongst the other travellers who moved to and fro upon that mighty highway, and the bright, winter sunshine shone down on them, making the sea sparkle with reflected silver.

'The world!' cried Huillam D'Averc in considerable relish. 'At last, at last, the world!'

Hawkmoon found D'Averc's joy infectious. 'Where do you go? To Londra or the Kamarg?'

'To Londra, of course, at once!' said D'Averc. 'After all, a kingdom awaits me.'

'You were never a cynic, Huillam D'Averc,' said Yisselda of Brass, 'and you cannot make us think you are one now. Give our greetings to Queen Flana. Tell her we shall visit her soon.'

Huillam D'Averc bowed with a flourish. 'And my greetings, in turn, to your father, Count Brass. Tell him I shall be sitting beside his fire before long and drinking his wine. Is the castle as draughty as it ever was?'

'We shall prepare a room suitable for one of your delicate health,' Yisselda told him. She took the hand of her son Manfred and the hand of her daugher Yarmila. For the first time, she noticed that Yarmila was holding something. It was Jhary-a-Conel's small black and white cat.

'Master Fank gave it to me, mother,' said the child.

'Treat it well, then,' said her father, 'for it is a rarity, that little beast.'

'Farewell for the moment, Huillam D'Averc,' said Bowgentle. 'I found most interesting the time we spent in Limbo.'

'I, too, Master Bowgentle. Though I still wish we had had that deck of cards.' Again, the dandy bowed. 'And good-bye, Oladahn, smallest of giants. I wish I could listen to your boastings when you return to the Kamarg.'

'They would be no match for yours, sir, I fear.' Oladahn stroked his whiskers, pleased with the retort. 'I look forward to your visit.'

Hawkmoon began to stride forward along the shining roadway, eager to begin the journey back to Castle Brass, where the children would meet their noble old grandfather.

'We'll purchase horses at Karlye,' he said. 'We have credit there.' He turned to his son. 'Tell me, Manfred, what do you remember of your adventures?' He tried to disguise a certain anxiety for his son. 'Do you remember a great deal?'

'No, father,' said Manfred kindly. 'I remember very

143

little.' And he ran forward, and, taking his father's hand, led him towards the distant shore.

This ends the Third and Last of the Chronicles of Castle Brass

This ends the long story of the Eternal Champion

Michael Moorcock in paperback from Grafton Books

The Cornelius Chronicles
The Adventures of Una Persson and Catherine Cornelius
   in the Twentieth Century   £2.50 ☐

The Dancers at the End of Time
An Alien Heat   £1.25 ☐
The Hollow Lands   £1.50 ☐
The End of All Songs   £1.95 ☐
The Dancers at the End of Time (omnibus)   £3.50 ☐

Hawkmoon: The History of the Runestaff
The Jewel in the Skull   £1.95 ☐
The Mad God's Amulet   £1.95 ☐
The Sword of the Dawn   £1.95 ☐
The Runestaff   £1.95 ☐
The History of the Runestaff (omnibus)   £2.95 ☐

Hawkmoon: The Chronicles of Castle Brass
Count Brass   £1.50 ☐
The Champion of Garathorm   £1.95 ☐
The Quest for Tanelorn   £1.25 ☐

Erekosë
The Eternal Champion   £1.95 ☐
Phoenix in Obsidian   £1.95 ☐

Elric
The Sailor on the Seas of Fate   £1.95 ☐
The Weird of the White Wolf   £1.95 ☐
The Vanishing Tower   £2.50 ☐
The Bane of the Black Sword   £1.95 ☐
Stormbringer   £1.95 ☐

The Books of Corum
The Knight of the Swords   £1.95 ☐
The Queen of the Swords   £1.95 ☐
The King of the Swords   £1.95 ☐
The Bull and the Spear   £2.50 ☐
The Oak and the Ram   £2.50 ☐
The Sword and the Stallion   £1.95 ☐

Oswald Bastable
The War Lord of the Air   £1.50 ☐
The Land Leviathan   £1.50 ☐
The Steel Tsar   £1.25 ☐
The Nomad of Time (omnibus)   £2.95 ☐

SF1181

The world's greatest science fiction authors now available in paperback from Grafton Books

Bob Shaw

One Million Tomorrows	£1.50	☐
A Better Mantrap	£1.50	☐
Orbitsville	£1.95	☐
Orbitsville Departure	£1.95	☐
Fire Pattern	£1.95	☐
The Palace of Eternity	£2.50	☐

Arthur C Clarke

1984: Spring (non-fiction)	£2.50	☐
The Sentinel	£2.95	☐
2010 Odyssey Two	£1.95	☐

Harry Harrison

West of Eden	£2.50	☐
Skyfall	£2.50	☐
Captive Universe	£1.50	☐
You Can be the Stainless Steel Rat: An Interactive Game Book	£1.95	☐
Rebel in Time	£2.50	☐

'To The Stars' Trilogy

Homeworld	£1.95	☐
Wheelworld	£1.95	☐
Starworld	£2.50	☐

Doris Lessing
'Canopus in Argos: Archives'

Shikasta	£2.95	☐
The Marriage Between Zones Three, Four, and Five	£2.50	☐
The Sirian Experiments	£2.95	☐
The Making of the Representative for Planet 8	£2.50	☐
Documents Relating to the Sentimental Agents in the Volyen Empire	£2.50	☐

David Mace

Demon 4	£1.95	☐
Nightrider	£1.95	☐
Firelance	£2.50	☐

To order direct from the publisher just tick the titles you want and fill in the order form.

The world's greatest science fiction authors now available in paperback from Grafton Books

To order direct from the publisher just tick the titles you want and fill in the order form.   **SF1382**

Isaac Asimov, grand master of science fiction now available in paperback from Grafton Books

'Foundation' Series

Foundation	£1.95	☐
Foundation and Empire	£1.95	☐
Second Foundation	£2.50	☐
Foundation's Edge	£2.95	☐

Other Titles

Opus: The Best of Isaac Asimov	£2.50	☐
The Bicentennial Man	£1.95	☐
Buy Jupiter!	£1.95	☐
The Gods Themselves	£1.95	☐
The Early Asimov (Volume 1)	£1.50	☐
The Early Asimov (Volume 2)	£1.50	☐
The Early Asimov (Volume 3)	£1.50	☐
Earth`is Room Enough	£1.95	☐
The Stars Like Dust	£1.95	☐
The Martian Way	£1.50	☐
The Currents of Space	£1.50	☐
Nightfall One	£1.50	☐
Nightfall Two	£1.95	☐
The End of Eternity	£1.95	☐
I, Robot	£1.95	☐
The Rest of the Robots	£1.95	☐
The Complete Robot	£3.50	☐
Asimov's Mysteries	£2.50	☐
The Caves of Steel	£1.95	☐
The Naked Sun	£1.95	☐
The Robots of Dawn	£2.50	☐
Nebula Award Stories 8 (Editor)	95p	☐
The Stars in their Courses (non-fiction)	£1.50	☐
Asimov's Guide to Halley's Comet (non-fiction)	£2.50	☐
Counting the Eons (non-fiction)	£2.50	☐
Asimov on Science Fiction (non-fiction)	£2.50	☐
X Stands for Unknown (non-fiction)	£2.95	☐

To order direct from the publisher just tick the titles you want and fill in the order form.

The world's greatest science fiction authors now available in paperback from Grafton Books

Ursula K LeGuin

The Dispossessed	£2.50	☐
The Lathe of Heaven	£1.95	☐
Threshold	£1.95	☐

Short Stories

Orsinian Tales	£1.50	☐
The Wind's Twelve Quarters (Volume 1)	£1.25	☐
The Wind's Twelve Quarters (Volume 2)	£1.25	☐

Ursula K LeGuin and Others

The Eye of the Heron	£1.95	☐

A E van Vogt

The Voyage of the Space Beagle	£2.50	☐
The Book of Ptath	£1.95	☐
Destination Universe!	£1.50	☐

To order direct from the publisher just tick the titles you want and fill in the order form.   SF481

The world's greatest science fiction authors now available in paperback from Grafton Books

J G Ballard

The Crystal World	£2.50	☐
The Drought	£2.50	☐
Hello America	£2.50	☐
The Disaster Area	£2.50	☐
Crash	£2.50	☐
Low-Flying Aircraft	£2.50	☐
The Atrocity Exhibition	£2.50	☐
The Venus Hunters	£2.50	☐
The Day of Forever	£2.50	☐
The Unlimited Dream Company	£2.50	☐
Concrete Island	£2.50	☐
Myths of the Near Future	£2.50	☐
High Rise	£2.50	☐

Philip Mann

The Eye of the Queen	£1.95	☐

To order direct from the publisher just tick the titles you want and fill in the order form.

SF581

The world's greatest science fiction authors now available in paperback from Grafton Books

Ray Bradbury

Fahrenheit 451	£2.50	☐
The Small Assassin	£2.50	☐
The October Country	£1.50	☐
The Illustrated Man	£1.95	☐
The Martian Chronicles	£1.95	☐
Dandelion Wine	£2.50	☐
The Golden Apples of the Sun	£1.95	☐
Something Wicked This Way Comes	£2.50	☐
The Machineries of Joy	£1.50	☐
Long After Midnight	£1.95	☐
The Stories of Ray Bradbury (Volume 1)	£3.95	☐
The Stories of Ray Bradbury (Volume 2)	£3.95	☐

Philip K Dick

Flow My Tears, The Policeman Said	£2.50	☐
Blade Runner (Do Androids Dream of Electric Sheep?)	£1.95	☐
Now Wait for Last Year	£1.95	☐
The Zap Gun	£1.95	☐
A Handful of Darkness	£1.50	☐
A Maze of Death	£2.50	☐
Ubik	£1.95	☐
Our Friends from Frolix 8	£1.95	☐
Clans of the Alphane Moon	£1.95	☐
The Transmigration of Timothy Archer	£2.50	☐
A Scanner Darkly	£1.95	☐
The Three Stigmata of Palmer Eldrich	£1.95	☐
The Penultimate Truth	£1.95	☐
We Can Build You	£2.50	☐

To order direct from the publisher just tick the titles you want and fill in the order form. **SF981**

All these books are available at your local bookshop or newsagent, or can be ordered direct from the publisher.

To order direct from the publishers just tick the titles you want and fill in the form below.

Name _____

Address _____

_____

Send to:
Grafton Cash Sales
PO Box 11, Falmouth, Cornwall TR10 9EN.

Please enclose remittance to the value of the cover price plus:

UK 60p for the first book, 25p for the second book plus 15p per copy for each additional book ordered to a maximum charge of £1.90.

BFPO 60p for the first book, 25p for the second book plus 15p per copy for the next 7 books, thereafter 9p per book.

Overseas including Eire £1.25 for the first book, 75p for second book and 28p for each additional book.

Grafton Books reserve the right to show new retail prices on covers, which may differ from those previously advertised in the text or elsewhere.